EVERYONE ON MARS

EVERYONE ON MARS

STORIES FROM THE RED SHIFT

LARRY BUTTROSE

PUNCHER & WATTMANN

First published in 2024
Published by Puncher and Wattmann
PO Box 279
Waratah NSW 2298

https://www.puncherandwattmann.com
web@puncherandwattmann.com

ISBN   9781923099180

Edited by Ed Wright
Cover design by Miranda Douglas
Typesetting by Morgan Arnett
Printed by Lightning Source International

A catalogue record for this work is available from the National Library of Australia

This project has been assisted by the Australian Government through Creative Australia, its principal arts investment and advisory body.

This book is dedicated to my children, Jack and Ada.

My sincere thanks to Blazenka Brysha, who so generously reads every word I write, and has given invaluable feedback on this book; Geri Johnstone, the first reader of these stories, who urged me to go on with them; my dear friend Donna Maegraith with her forensic editorial eye; Niobe Syme for her critical insight and gracious editorial assistance; and my agent Virginia Lloyd, for her belief.

The Baroness was first published by the Rochford Street Review.

Contents

Writer in Residence

The books had been a problem. But she had insisted. Four months without her Woolf and Joyce, Allende and Plath, Dostoyevsky and Marquez were not possible. They weren't fancy editions, most were mass-market paperbacks, which made it all the more difficult to explain to them. Electronic books are not authentic books, she said. They argued they were the same thing, just text stored in a different way. No, she said. The medium truly is the message. Electronic books are as ineffable as the ideas they come from: they lack the authority and truth of print stamped into paper, something you can touch and hold and that will never alter. Turn the gadget off and where are the e-books? But a real book, silent and motionless as a cat on a shelf, is a thing of beauty. Novels, stories, poems are wellsprings of our human wisdom and delight, she told them. When you hold a copy of *To The Lighthouse*, that's what you feel. It's not to do with the intellect: it is life between two covers. But they're heavy, they argued, they'll take up room. So it came down to how heavy and how many, and she had packed her few dozen non-negotiable books, the ones she ran her fingers down now, and the spines shivered.

She flicked back through her manuscript over coffee. Something nagged about Carlos. Could he really be that offhand about his mother's diagnosis, just because Julia had never liked her? Was he that suggestible, guileless and cruel? That wasn't his whole story but it was part of it. She sipped and wondered if there was enough of the mother in the second chapter, and of Julia's secret girlfriend in the third, and whether it was too much that they were caught up in political treachery too. She drank down the rest of the coffee. God, how had she come to write such dross? Yet it was the kind of thing her publisher said her readers wanted, and from meeting them at festivals, she knew it was true. She glanced up at her little shelf of books. She was yet to write one she could even hope to place near them, and after her early grit, fire and phosphorescence, probably never would now. She'd had the freedom back then. Past the shelf was her window and her eye was drawn as ever to the distant range in all its hazy orange-red, then to the smooth-topped little hill that overlooked the colony, and now to the black rocks in the dirt just outside. Martian hills, Martian rocks. Mars. She was really on Mars.

He could not believe he was going to meet her. He might have fantasised back on Earth, but here of all places it was really going to happen. 'Mila Avila,' he said out loud to himself. *Mila. Avila.* He entered her domus with circumspection and found her in the greenhouse amid sprung rows of carrots and beets. She was sitting on a trail chair, looking at what he wasn't sure.

'Oh. Sorry.'

She looked up. 'What for?'

'Interrupting you.'

'From what?'

'Whatever you were doing.'

'I wasn't doing anything.'

'I'm Jason Forno. We have an appointment.'

She didn't move. 'Thank you for being on time.'

He fidgeted a little and looked around. 'I like your snake plants… Sansevieria,' he said, pointing to the pair of potted ornamentals on stands. 'Beautiful, aren't they? And they seem to like the decontam.'

'I'm still surprised any non-edibles are allowed on Mars.'

'Yeah, well, "mental wellness" is big here.'

'And I'm still trying to get my head around eating anything grown here… wondering how decontaminated the decontam is anyway.'

'It works pretty well. I love snake plants even if we can't eat them. They're so wilful, determined. Hardy, don't need too much water.'

'What do you do here?'

'Maintenance,' he said. 'Mining robotics.'

'I didn't know there was mining.'

'There's some.'

'For what.'

'Different things.'

'For here? Or Earth?'

'For Earth it'd have to be just about as precious and small as diamonds to make it worthwhile getting back there. No, it's really for here. Construction, you name it, everything.'

'Do you enjoy it?'

'Every day I wonder how I got here doing this. I just want to write now. That's all I want to do. All I ever really have.'

'Half of humanity wants to write. It's another thing to do it. So what have you brought me? A draft? I haven't seen anything from you.'

'I really just wanted to talk to you about how you work. I've read all your books. I'm a huge fan.'

'Please don't say that. Coffee? Tea?'

'Coffee, please.'

She got up. From her books he'd imagined her taller.

'You're American,' she said.

'From Indiana, the Hoosier state. Indianapolis. Like Kurt Vonnegut… Bokonon. Poo-tee-weet. Insanity is contagious.'

'You know I'm from Cuba. We could almost be enemies.'

'Even weirder at this distance, isn't it.'

She shrugged and led him into the kitchen alcove and opened a fresh jar of coffee.

'I've been writing in my head all my life,' he said. 'But when I finish it, the story I'm writing now will be my first completed work.'

'As someone said, it takes you your whole life to learn to write, and then you die.'

He grinned. 'Lucky I'm starting early then.'

'Milk with your coffee? I don't know if I have any.'

'That's OK.'

She started making it and he wandered over towards her shelf.

'Books,' he marvelled. 'Real books.'

'Yes.'

'May I touch them?'

'Not yet.'

By far the hardest part was the reading. Presumably the idea of a writer in residence was for the "wellness" – she could barely think such a disgusting word – of the colonists. And to give the visiting writers vistas and moments of a lifetime. She had been out two or three times "suited up" in the surface vehicles that tracked the wastes around ElonGate. It reminded her of the Atacama in Chile, or Sturt's Stony Desert in Australia. From the rum-sweated grime of Havana to the trash cans and bums sleeping by her door on Canal Street, here was the glory of a clean, cold and dry nothingness. If life had ever been here, it was long gone, leaving an empty place of such majesty it wailed.

She read diligently through the stories on her screen as a deal was a deal and she considered it a point of honour to acquit. Many were love letters to the blue and green planet they missed, with romantic portraits of thinly veiled lovers and spouses back home, and sentimental ones of mothers and fathers, even pets. Others depicted life on Mars as a drudgery, if in words it was drudgery to read. She had asked for a work profile of the colonists and it came back that most were scientists and engineers, maintenance workers, medical staff, computer wonks and bio and botanical geeks. There were machinists and emergency crews, and the carers and teachers of the first native-born Martian humans. There were the drivers and pilots, some she presumed must work in the Closed Module, about whom little was ever said. She was intrigued to know there were miners here too, who it seemed must be categorised under the blanket term "technicians".

The day she saw Jason Forno's story appear on her screen, from its

4

opening sentence she knew it was very different from all the others. It was about a young man dispatched by his company to work on Mars, who decided there had to be more to life than the sum of his shifts. As she read on, a kind of existentialist Martian rebel began to emerge, a young man who in his down time chose not to drink beers in the Mess, but who went off alone into the wastes, scaling hills, exploring ravines and crannies, and testing as he does so the limit of his oxygen supply. Once he had arrived back on his very last breath. "It was exhilarating, it made it feel real." But ever more disillusioned, soon the unnamed character starts engaging in meaningless antisocial acts. He scratches obscene graffiti on distant rocks and spells out "Fuck Mars" in a giant, painstaking arrangement of stones, among other petty and rather silly acts. As time goes by he engages in minor vandalism, breaking a canteen coffee machine and dropping delicate equipment accidentally on purpose.

No-one puts one and one together. But after shorting a generator he realises he's going too far, from simple pointlessness to being a danger to others. He decides then to act on something that's been simmering in his back-brain. He suits up and treks to the top of the nearest hill, the smooth-topped one with the panoramic view of the grid of the colony and the space port beyond. The temperature has fallen to nearly minus 70 Celsius overnight but is now an almost balmy 3 Celsius outside his suit.

"He stood looking down over ElonGate, contemplating the thriving little settlement on the plain, and all humanity had achieved here, making its species truly bi-planetary. And yet for what, he thought. Just another planet to mess up as badly as our beautiful cripple, the Earth? Was that all? People on Earth had asked themselves for millennia 'Why am I here?' Surely that same question must whisper, rise and boom down the canyons of Mars.

"By a complex set of hacks and overrides, he was able to remove his helmet. The cold was deep and intense, and made him feel very alert. 'One, two, three…' and he inhaled. He knew it was nearly all carbon dioxide with almost no oxygen and he had only a few seconds until he blacked out, and his heart broke on this meaningless outcrop of rock.

But he had never felt more alive. He breathed out and in again, painfully. 'Four, five, six... seven...' Perhaps he could go on, he suddenly thought. Perhaps he could breathe here, after all. Perhaps he was already transmuting into a Martian.

"Then he felt the daggers inside and his consciousness was suddenly fading, and knew he had perhaps two seconds to get his helmet back on. He fumbled with it."

The story ended there.

She knew well which hill and scaled it as quickly as she could. She glimpsed the shape on the ground at the summit and knew what it was. His bared head protruded from his suit as he lay on his back by the discarded helmet on the pebbles and sand, wide eyes staring up toward the stars, and he was smiling.

After all the recovery arrangements and officialdom had been dealt with, she returned to her domus and sat for a long time in the greenhouse looking at what he had told her were called snake plants. She saw now how wondrous were these ever upward probing tendrils of green. She felt they were the real reason humans were there. Sitting on her trail chair nursing a brandy, she took out an envelope with her name hand-written on it, "Mila Avila", with a curlicue beneath it. The paper felt alive in her fingertips. Shaking a little, she opened the note inside and read.

"Dear Ms Avila. It was my profound privilege and pleasure to meet you. I hope I learnt how to write in my lifetime, at least a little. It would be a waste otherwise, don't you think? And may I touch your books now, please? They are the most beautiful things I've ever seen. Even more beautiful than you, who would never think in such terms, but you are, along with every word you have ever written. Sincerely, Jason Forno."

The Law

The daily case list was short. It nearly always was. That shouldn't be surprising: with only a few thousand highly educated, skilled, and well paid inhabitants, you might not expect a lot. As Chief Magistrate, in fact the only magistrate, it was my job to officiate in the cases our tiny law enforcement unit saw fit to bring before me. Nearly all were minor matters: drunken tomfoolery, common assault and affray, petty theft, the occasional scrawl of graffiti and so on, although sometimes there were more serious cases, of sexual misconduct and domestic violence, and these did seem on the rise. Some of them were very sad as quarters were close and any disturbance all too obvious. Many preferred to suffer on in silence. A sociologist had remarked that some residents of ElonGate endured a "tyranny of quiet", feeling they could not just "have it out" like couples did back on Earth. Mental health was increasingly an issue, and more experts were being sent to Mars. There were all kinds of weird rumours too, one being that the settlement's radiation insulation was insufficient, which was leading to cognitive impairment, despite official denials. I had even heard one bizarre theory that Mars, the red planet of anger and war, could by its essence make people more likely to turn violent, even if that one had been shot down with statistics about how people behaved in small communities in tough, isolated places back on Earth. Harsh conditions make for hard people, the conventional wisdom went. Fortunately for me, all I had to do was judge on the matters of law and leave the theorising to those so disposed.

Or at least so I thought until the day Nin Pravat came before me. I had already imposed fines on a couple of drunks and a listed-substance offender, and even sent one habitual type to brief detention in our "chokey". It was little different from our living quarters, small and basic, only people couldn't leave or draw pay while inside. It wasn't much of a deterrent, but then there wasn't much crime.

But the case involving Nin was a different matter. For one thing, she had brought the action herself. Civil cases were far rarer than police matters. The few businesses on Mars we had were yet to get involved in commercial disputes. We had not a single defamation action. Divorces were handled pro forma for the most part: the parties signed with one of the two practising solicitors, and it was settled with a digital stamp from me.

Divorce sparked Nin Pravat's action. She was a petite, rather retiring woman, Thai, a doctor. She had arrived alone but within a few months married Lotta, a Finn she met in the Mess. I officiated at their nuptials myself. But the relationship seemed not to have worked out. Lotta was constantly away on a team drilling core samples for a mining company. The fire died in the lonely months. Nin decided the marriage was not for her and after the statutory year, she applied for divorce. However, Lotta remained stubbornly in love with her and did not want to let her go just like that. She said she wanted more time to try to save the marriage: but Nin wanted her freedom and now. Under the law she was within her rights to have it, and so she brought the case before me. It was essentially procedural.

Lotta was substantially larger than life, long-limbed, milk-and-honey skinned with a bird's nest of blond dreads. Both women were intriguing in their own way and in different circumstances I would have enjoyed sitting down to dine with them together, or with either of them alone. But these were not those circumstances. Nin wanted out, and Lotta wanted to avert that in any way she could, although why she would want to remain with a partner who clearly did not want her any more was hard for me to comprehend. Had Jean wanted a divorce, I would have said "just go". But Lotta was Lotta, and no-one else but Lotta, and when I thought about it more, I didn't really know what I would do if Jean asked me. I suppose none of us knows what we might do in tough enough circumstances. We seem so sovereign and strong until put to the test, and then, well, I suppose we find out who we really are. All piss and wind, most of us discover.

They sat at tables on either side of the courtroom. Nin sat beside her lawyer, Thomas Tonks, something of a dandy and "young man around ElonGate." Lotta sat alone at the other table, head down writing notes. After I made my entrance and all had stood and sat down, I called upon Mr Tonks to put the case.

'In the simplest of terms, Madam Magistrate, my client Nin Pravat wants a divorce from Lotta Salo. The couple married just over a year ago. Now Ms Pravat wants a divorce but Ms Salo has refused to sign the agreement, and that has brought us here. There is no legal impediment to the divorce being finalised. The required no-fault period has passed. There are no dependants, nor financial issues of any size to be resolved. All that is needed is the signature of Ms Salo, which she refuses to give, and that has brought us before you to dissolve the union by order.'

'Thank you, Mr Tonks,' I said. 'Ms Salo, do you have any reason why I should not issue the order immediately?'

Lotta Salo stood to speak. As mentioned she was a substantial woman, and in her own way beautiful. She had an enigmatic allure I could see might have attracted the eye of the obviously more reserved Nin in the first place. She was wearing a simple sky-blue shift and low heels, but it was hard for anyone including also Nin herself, and Tonks too, to take their eyes off her.

'Madam Magistrate, may I call you that too?' she asked.

'Of course. That is my title.'

'May I approach for a word please?'

'Very well.'

She did so, approaching so closely I could smell her breath. Despite the reputation some Finns might have back on Earth, it did not smell of anything but sweet mint. Her eyes were a sea green you could wish to sail.

'Yes, Ms Salo?'

'You are a woman yourself,' she said softly.

'When I last looked. Why?'

'Have you ever felt a love you thought could only be wrenched out of you together with your beating heart?'

'That is just the nature of love, Ms Salo.'

'But you see the danger.'

'My own spouse doesn't wish to divorce me, so that is not the issue. You are. Now what do you wish to say to me?'

'I ask you Madam Magistrate, from what or whom does this court draw its authority?'

'Pardon?'

'Whose authority permits you to make judgements in this court?'

'This court as you well know operates under the mandate of the United Nations.'

'Which was given after the planet was first colonised by a private company.'

'That's correct. But what's your point? I need to get on with things here.'

'Tell me where are these United Nations, Madam Magistrate?'

I sighed to show my growing frustration. 'We both know they are on Earth, Ms Salo.'

She nodded. 'Thank you. That is all I needed to hear. Excuse me.' She returned to the table where she had been sitting, and took a jar filled with red soil from her bag. She held it up high for all in the courtroom to see.

'This is the soil of our planet, Mars!' she declared. 'We are not on planet Earth anymore! We are living here. We are Martians. And the laws of a distant blue dot in our sky no longer have any bearing on our red planet home.'

There was a puzzled silence in the courtroom. A few seconds passed. Nin gave Tonks a look, and his eyes turned to me and I nodded.

'So,' I said, 'just for clarification Ms Salo, are you suggesting you intend to challenge the legal jurisdiction of this court, conferred by the United Nations, and Earth itself, over the settlement of ElonGate?'

'Let me put it like this Madam Magistrate. In 100, 200 years or so we may well be self-sufficient on this planet, possibly even sooner. We Martians will not need Earth any more. The so-called rights of Earth will be history by then. Who knows, one day in the distant future, if things are mishandled as badly as humans are prone to do, there could even be a real war of the worlds.'

I was starting to suspect by now why Nin was so keen to finalise the divorce promptly.

'So… you're telling me your case to stop me granting a divorce, rests on this.'

'Yes. And when you think about it, there's nothing greater. Why should we obey an entity on a distant foreign planet? I challenge the United Nations mandate. Mars is a free world, will be in the future, and always will be. Just as my love for Nin always will be. I celebrate its beginning and I will not see its end. I love her and I will never let her go, as I swore on my soul to do the day we wed. As did Nin.'

She stopped speaking and looked toward Nin, who avoided her eyes and looked down.

'Madam Magistrate,' Lotta went on, 'are you aware of the Outer Space Treaty of 1967?'

'I am. There is a copy of it in the court library.'

'And are you aware that was an agreement to give no spacefaring nation sovereignty over any extra-terrestrial body, including the Earth's moon, asteroids and the planets?'

'I am.'

'So what then is this United Nations, from which you derive your authority in this courtroom? It is an international body, composed of the nations of the world. But those nations have divested themselves of territorial authority in space. And as the United Nations is just that, those and other similar nations united, surely it, like its constituents, is also divested of territorial authority in space. So I ask you again, upon whom or what does your authority in this court legitimately rely?'

'I am also aware,' I replied, 'as you no doubt are too, that the UN is currently establishing the Mars Territorial Authority that will be the legitimate body in charge here, with a leader and a cabinet, with three of its members elected by the community.'

'Which it has been establishing for years… and hasn't managed to yet, because of disputes over mineral rights, and over any life forms we may yet find here. Which means that as of this moment, your position still has no legitimacy.'

There was plainly audible frustration and an impatient shifting in the court now, and I knew I had to finish with this.

'Ms Salo, in the end all authority derives from convention. In the Middle Ages it was whichever warlord had control and could call himself king. Now it's national elected governments, or countries ruled on the whims of dictators. The authority of the United Nations is as strong as one can get, or one practically needs.'

Tonks had been becoming increasingly annoyed about all this and finally rose, his patience at an end, but his voice was as ever suave as the cut of his suit. His lustrous brown hair fell just so across his brow, and his eyes were bright as Sirius. 'This is an absurdity your honour. Please just make the ruling now so that it's settled and we can all go.'

It was a fair call and I gave it due consideration and was on the point of complying. But something nagged. Despite my spiel about conventions, what Lotta had said was true for now, even if it involved a little logical leap-frogging, and failed to recognise that in the early days of any colony, the law may exercise latitude in the cause of what is practical and possible.

'A private word please,' I said to Lotta. 'Court adjourned for 15 minutes.'

I saw a look of surprise on the face of Tonks, who then quickly turned and reassured Nin, whose own face remained steadfastly down.

I went to my chambers and Lotta was shown in.

'So you think you've found a loophole, Ms Salo.'

'I don't think I have. I know it. And now I'll be seeking a judgement on it from the highest court on this planet. You.'

'You know I can't go against the UN mandate.'

'Why not?'

'Common sense for one thing. Just say we were to try to declare our legal or any other kind of independence from Earth. If our current Administrator said we were now our own entity, on Earth they'd think it a joke at first and a psychological disturbance next. We can't survive without Earth here, not now and maybe never, despite what you think. We are at the disposal of those who sent us here.'

'That may be true, certainly for the foreseeable future, I admit. But it doesn't make it right. And ultimately at this very moment you have no true legitimacy for the power you wield here.'

'Other than necessity. Other than we need the rule of law here and someone needs to administer justice, and it's turned out that someone is me.'

'I can lodge this as a formal legal challenge.'

'Of course you can. And I'll have to dismiss it. And you'll appeal and I'll dismiss that too. You could try to appeal to Earth but they'd just think you're a troublemaking lunatic.' I stopped and looked at her. 'Why don't we talk about you and Nin.'

She considered. 'All right.'

'Why won't you accept what she wants?'

She hesitated. 'I never thought it would be me saying this. But vulnerable people are even more so here. I mean, who'd want to be alone here? What do I see every day when I'm out there working? There's nothing here. Nothing but some minerals under its surface. This is a frontier mining town,' she said. 'With sharks like Tonks circling for prey.'

I thought a moment. 'What don't I know about this?'

'I think Tonks is behind it.'

'Are they involved?'

'I don't know.'

'Is she bisexual?'

'Nin is insecure. She has family money back on Earth. Plenty of it. And predators like him feed on women like her. And ever since she went to him to discuss our position, she's gone harder and harder, and here we are.'

'She's of course within her rights to get a divorce.'

'I don't dispute that. I'm not a nut or an emotional fascist. But I think there's a lot more to this. I think she's being manipulated. Look at her. She can barely make eye contact.'

It was true. I have observed many people in courtrooms and her body language was plain. There was something she did not wish to be aired. But in this case, the law did not require that.

'Even if that's true, it's still up to her isn't it.'

'Yes. But if she was properly engaged with reality, in her right mind, I don't think she'd be doing anything like this. You do know, don't you, there's a silent epidemic of mental illness here. No-one can take it here. Especially alone. And many people who are with someone are terrified it will all just go to hell and they'll be left alone.'

'You think she's off the rails? Or that she really loves you still?'

'We made love last night. And the night before that. Etcetera.'

I sat forward. 'So why does she want a divorce then?'

'He's controlling her.'

'Do you have any proof?'

'Not that would stand up in court.'

'Then I have to grant her a divorce. Today. And you can appeal and challenge my jurisdiction if you want to.'

She said nothing at first. 'No. I won't do that. I just wanted you to listen to me. There's so much going on here, subterranean stuff, that you people in charge seem not to be noticing.'

'Well I'm glad you've mentioned it. And I'm sorry to have to do it. But it's the law.'

'I know. But whose law? His? Earth's? Or ours?'

'For now it's just the law.'

Jean wasn't home when I got back. The hours in the lab were never-ending. I messaged but didn't get a reply, as often happened. I made dinner and drank a glass or two. I sat on the sofa in front of the screen and thought about what Lotta had said. Had Nin been manipulated by Tonks? Well, everyone in ElonGate knew Tonks spent plenty of money. I thought about the mandate under which I operated: Lotta was techni-cally right, and she or someone else could and might challenge it. Not that they could win. I sat there thinking, but more than anything else

14

I sat there wondering when Jean would come home. It was true this was not the kind of place anyone would ever wish to be alone. It could maim the soul even of a woman like Lotta.

A Horse with Good Manners

Mercifully the midwinter day wasn't too hot and sultry as I stepped outside after my lunch meeting. I was about to jump into a cab back to the office when something flashed in the afternoon sunlight and lured my eye. With intrigued steps I approached a store display window. It was huge and framed with what looked like dark lacquered wood, real. I had forgotten such a thing existed. Peering in, I saw my reflection in the plate glass, and a memory started to form, of Christmas time, when my parents would take me out to see the city's tree, decorations and lights, and the displays in illuminated windows of the department stores. I remembered seeing a jet suspended in clouds of cotton wool, a toy International Space Station orbiting a beachball globe, a rocket zooming through space against a black velvet backdrop studded with pin lights of stars, cellophane flames leaping from its thrusters. My parents would ask me what I wanted from the window and I would say 'everything!', and they would laugh in a good natured ho-ho-ho, and my father would put his arm around me and my mother's warm kiss would bless my brow, and I would think "this is what it must be like to be a happy family... so we must be a happy family". Which we were, in a way, if it seldom felt like it. My father was mostly away with work, and when I got home from school my mother would be tired out from running her online business and already into the wine, and I would go upstairs and do my homework and get onto my devices, and other than dinner, that was our day done. But Christmas was different. When we looked into that big department store window I would see the reflections of the three of us laughing there, and for that moment I could think "happy family". And I would inevitably get the biggest and best thing I asked for, the latest rocket. By the time I turned thirteen I had an entire launch range set up in my room.

The thing I saw in the display window now wasn't a rocket though. It was a boxed plastic model you assembled with glue. A kit. Remarkable, I thought. Maybe there's a retro modelling fad now. Or perhaps it never completely died out, and I'd just forgotten about such things and it had taken until now to be reminded they were still out there. I saw the store entrance, looking much like it always had, and with no urgent need to get back to work, I was tempted to go in.

I passed beneath the copperplate "Benson Brothers" sign and through the grand revolving door. Stepping inside, I was greeted by soft light, quiet and calm. Everything was meticulously ordered in brass and glass cases and laid out on shelves, with wares that looked finely crafted and worth owning. There was no trace of the disposable stuff of the now, bought one day and junked the next. Was I dreaming? I looked back out through the entrance to where the pod cabs swarmed. No, that all looked here and now enough, as did the fashions displayed on the mannequins in the store. Somehow Benson Brothers must have remained here all along, open and trading, and so many years had come and gone and left it almost untouched. The now was now all right, but here I stood in my past.

I approached a counter. The assistant was a young woman in the store's black uniform with coiffed blond curls and a mouth like a fresh strawberry. 'Yes, sir? How can I help?'

'I don't get to this part of town often, miss, and I... I just can't...' I stammered, feeling a little foolish, '...I can't believe this place is still here, and just like it was in my childhood. Even the big display windows on the street look exactly the same.'

'Yes sir, we do get this quite a lot,' she nodded. 'Benson Brothers has never changed. We still provide the same standards of service, product quality and range, and the classic interior of our store remains as it always has been. Benson Brothers prides itself on its traditions and enduring standards, because our motto is...'

A rusty mental cog somewhere clanked. 'Elegance... discretion and service?'

She smiled with teeth so white they almost hurt my eyes. 'Yes sir, that's absolutely right. Are you certain it's that long since your last visit?'

'I… haven't been here since I was a boy. But it doesn't seem to have changed, at all.'

I was struck by something else then. With her neat hair and red lipstick, the snug-fitting well cut black uniform and black seamed nylons with sensible heels, she looked exactly like the store attendants of my distant memory. When I was a kid coming here seamed stockings were already retro to the retro, and almost no-one who wasn't into cosplay had worn them in a very, very long time.

'Even you look the same… like the counter staff did back then,' I went on.

'Yes, sir. Some people even suspect odd things about that… that we're clones or something,' she said with a trilling little laugh, 'but I can assure you we're really just carefully recruited, trained and styled, so that the client may still enjoy the full, authentic Benson Brothers experience.'

'Are there… other stores… like this?'

'Of a similar authenticity, sir? Only a few, I believe. In London, Paris, Milan, New York. But here we are the only department store of our kind.'

'Extraordinary.'

It was indeed remarkable. I might have been standing here aged twelve again. But then something else came to mind. Who… who did she look like, in all her neat blond curls? A vintage film star, I thought. But it wasn't just a matter of her having "film star looks"… She reminded me of a particular star. But who? I racked through my movie memories, which happened to be quite extensive. This was because my grandparents had doted on the Golden Years of Hollywood, and especially on its great onscreen romantic couples… Fred Astaire and Ginger Rogers, Audrey Hepburn and Gregory Peck, Humphrey Bogart and Ingrid Bergman, Gloria Swanson and William Holden. They used to get me to watch the old movies over and again with them. It took a while for my teenage eyes to accept many of them, which were so ancient they were in black and white. But over time I got to like them almost as much as my grandparents did, and got so drawn into my favourites, like *All About Eve, What*

Ever Happened to Baby Jane? and *Sunset Boulevard*, that sometimes I had to pull back the curtains and look out through the window onto the street to remind myself I was still in this century.

For some reason my grandparents' favourite onscreen couple was June Allyson and James Stewart. June was the soft, quiet, ever-reassuring voice of conjugal love for "Jimmy". They did three movies together and we watched them over and over. *The Glenn Miller Story*, a baseball movie called *The Stratton Story*, and the Technicolor Cold War propaganda classic *Strategic Air Command*. I watched the two of them as a couple so often that I remembered them almost as well as my own parents. June Allyson's voice was a little deep, with a breathy, slightly rasping quality, but suffused with artful candour, and something else too: *I am with you darling. Fear not, you are warm and safe here with me.* She was the Hollywood star the woman behind the counter reminded me of.

'So now sir, how may I assist?' she said, jolting me back.

'Oh… well, in the window I see you have a model ElonGate kit.'

The words model and kit sounded so odd as I said them, especially linked to ElonGate, but she responded with her ever-ready smile. 'We do, yes. Would you like to see one?'

'Yes please.'

'And, who is the lucky recipient?'

'My son. Obsessed with space travel.'

'Aren't all children?' she laughed.

'He's especially so, I'd say.'

'Well space really is the thing nowadays, isn't it, more than ever.' She stopped, seemed to consider for a moment, then leaned in a little and spoke slightly more confidingly. Her skin smelled fresh as sea spray, her breath like lemon. 'My fiancé is up there. On Mars.' She said "fiancé" with a little country kind of twang that tingled.

'That must be rough for you.'

'I know fiancé is an old-fashioned word, and everyone these days has more modern ideas about marriage and relationships. But I wanted us to be engaged before he left.'

'But why not married?'

'Well… I think fiancé is a more romantic word than husband, don't you? "He's my fiancé" is so much sweeter than "he's my husband". Fiancé is the promise of the future. Which I think you need when you're going to be apart so long. While husband just sounds, well, shall we say, a bit less so.' She looked down. 'Oh, I'm sorry… I shouldn't be saying all this.'

'No,' I said. 'I mean, no, you should say it… if that's how you feel about the fiancé-husband thing.' I stopped. 'Actually, I wouldn't know. I'm at the other end of the sausage machine. I'm a widower.'

'Oh. I'm sorry to hear that, sir. And you seem such a nice man. Life isn't fair sometimes, is it?' She settled a stray blond strand. 'If you don't mind me asking, what is your line of work?'

'I'm in… insurance.'

'Well, we all need that too, don't we, especially with the way things are going.'

'We do.' I glanced around before I went on. 'Do you mind miss, if I ask your name?'

She grinned and pointed to a tag pinned to her chest. "Ali".

'How silly of me. Ali.'

'Not at all. It sometimes gets a bit covered up by my hair. I keep thinking maybe I should cut it to stop it happening.'

'Oh, no, please don't do that, don't cut it.'

She gave me a coy look. 'Why ever not, sir?'

'Because it's. Lovely.'

She positively blushed and lowered her voice a little further. 'I'm sorry sir. I've barely even spoken to a man since Jed left.'

'How long will he be there?'

'Another three years.' She squeezed a smile that crimped at the edges, and we both just stood there. I felt about as useful as a concrete pylon. But then I decided, what the hell, I can't just leave her with that, and threw caution to the proverbial wind. 'Would you perhaps consider coming out to dinner with me? Tonight?'

'Oh,' she said, with a tiny gasp, but smiling that smile anew. 'That's very nice of you to ask. But we're not meant to fraternise with customers. It's against Benson Brothers policy.'

I thought quickly. In insurance, there's always a loophole. 'But I haven't bought anything yet. So, I'm not strictly a customer yet.'

She leant in a fraction more. Around the corner of the counter I spied her ankle through the sheer of her stocking. It was a lovely ankle too, and her shoe dangled off her toes a little, in a manner that felt almost risqué.

'Well,' she considered. 'I suppose that's... strictly... true.' She thought a moment. 'Though, an account. Do you have one of those, as an established customer?'

'No I don't and I'm not. As I said, I didn't even realise the store was still here until now.'

She peered around the room and returned her hazy confiding eyes to mine. 'But I don't even know your name, sir.'

'Oh,' I said, suddenly flustered. 'I'm sorry.' I fastened my jacket button and stood up straight. 'It's...'

'Yes?'

'Well, it's...' I searched my brain. Every corner and crevice.

'You're just having a mental blank, sir. I get those all the time. Perhaps then what is your son's name? Often gentlemen in these parts name their sons after them.'

I thought again, searched again. I couldn't remember that either, my own son's name. Then, mercifully, it came to me.

'Bubba,' I said.

'Pardon?'

'My son's name is Bubba,' I grinned. 'Kind of a nickname.'

She laughed. 'So... dad...' she said, the shoe dangling by a thread now, 'could I call you Bubba too? As a... kind of nickname?'

'Yes, yes, of course,' and I laughed. 'Sorry. I must have just been...'

'Working too hard,' she said, and shook an ironic forefinger at me.

'Yes... I suppose so...'

'I'm sure you have been. People in a walk of life like yours always do. It must be very hard too, to have no-one to come home to now, to massage your neck and fix you a cocktail and then share a glass of wine with. That must be awful. And with a little boy too…' and on the blue-grey screen of her eyes I seemed to glimpse a little home with a tricycle in the front yard and a station wagon in the driveway. It was such an absurd fantasy I almost had to shake my head to return to my senses.

'How old is Bubba now?' she asked.

'Thirteen,' I said. 'So, will you join me for dinner tonight?'

Her voice was the purr of a cat in a lap. 'I'd be delighted.' Then she went on, 'and so now you can be the customer again,' and re-engaged her professional smile. 'Allow me to assist you with your request, sir.'

Husband and wife teams were fairly common in their branch of research, and in a way it suited officialdom to have them working in the field together. It could help things be more harmonious. They were drilling their fourth shaft for the day in search of what they thought to be a good chance of a significant body of underground ice. The other members of the team were in the next gorge with the vehicle, just over the rise.

Something made Masha look up. 'Uh oh,' she said.

'What is it?' He kept looking down at a sample they'd just brought to the surface.

'A big one… but nothing was forecast…'

He looked up and saw the approaching billow of dust. 'Jesus…'

The great red cloud reared towards them.

She had suggested we meet at Dino's. It was a little basement cocktail bar around the corner from Benson Brothers, down an alley that over time I had forgotten was there too. It had been a favourite night haunt for the city's "fast crowd" back in my grandparents' day, a hangout for politicians and movie starlets, crooners and models. I had been there a few times in my distant past, but seeing it again now, it seemed remarkably unchanged by the years, and I had the odd feeling of being an amateur archaeologist rediscovering my own hometown.

There was still the same subdued light I recalled, the wood panelling, the booths and the niches for two. The bartender was whistling a tune I couldn't quite make out, but thought I knew. I sat on a bar stool sipping a Manhattan, and was on the verge of asking him the tune when she came in. It was as if the room, the bar, the street outside, the very world witnessed her as one in that moment. She was a heart-racing, heart-stopping vision. Her flared shimmering dress was the green of young wheat rippling in the sun, wild and alive. Silk, simple, a la Dior New Look. Or perhaps it was the real thing, I couldn't tell any more. She needed little more than that, beyond a blue silk wrap around her shoulders, shoes and purse. All conversation stopped. Even the music seemed to fade, and only the whistling persisted, if softly now. She wore no visible adornments, and her hair fell in a way that kissed her bare arms while still allowing a peek of her milky back. Her neck was erect as a swan's, her eyes that powdery blue-grey, and her nose pert above all the lush redness of her mouth.

'*Volare*,' she said, kissing me on the cheek as I rose and helped her sit beside me.

'Pardon?'

'The tune the bartender's whistling. It's *Volare*. A lovely old, old song. It's Italian. It means to fly. And we all like that.'

'You look wonderful,' I said, forgetting to be surprised at her seeming to read my mind.

'As you look handsome. What's that you're having?'

'A Manhattan. Would you like one?'

'I'll take Manhattan too,' she smiled, and the bartender was already mixing it. 'They say that like life, it's the bitters that make it so good.' The bartender set it down before her and she put it to her lip-sticked lips and sipped. 'Very fancy on old Delancey.'

'You don't wear jewellery?' I said, and wondered as I did if it was somehow a faux pas.

'I don't like metal against my skin. Other than my dress, unmentionables and nylons, I'm naked as the day,' she laughed. 'Nice suit.' I looked

down and saw it was indeed quite a good one, charcoal, sharp cut. My
shirt had a pale blue stripe, and my tie was pale blue too.

'Thank you.'

'And I do love that tie,' she said. 'Like a distant sky before dusk.'

'It's the colour of your eyes,' I blurted out, saying it in the moment I
thought it, and then feeling like a fool.

'Is it? They change all the time. One day they're grey or greenish, the
next a kind of blue. I barely notice to tell you the truth. The mirror…
vanity, vanity, all is vanity,' she laughed.

She suggested we dine at Pellegrino's, next door. Again, I'd known it
once, a long time ago. She ate like a horse with good manners. She put
away a spaghetti vongole and a parmigiana while I just had grilled fish,
and then she ate a whole plate of gelato while I had a black coffee. We
also got through two bottles of a good valpolicella.

'Don't think I eat and drink like this all the time Bubba,' she joked.

When the others finally found them buried under the dust, they were
barely alive. The storm's winds were not powerful, but in seeking shelter
the pair had become disoriented and suffered falls, and their suits had
been damaged. Only the emergency defaults had kept their vital signs
going. Medical rescue drones were on the way, but after this amount of
time no-one knew if they would survive the journey back to ElonGate.

We wandered down darkened streets, with her showing me more land-
marks I seemed to have forgotten in this part of town. There were delis,
old pharmacies with shelves of giant jars, patent medicines, herbal remedies
and cosmetics, sawdust bars with happy drunks spilling out onto the street,
and shuck your own oyster places she said she wished she had the room
left to take me into. And via our meandering ways, we reached her door.

'It's been a wonderful night,' she breathed. 'One to remember.'

I smiled self-consciously. 'I've enjoyed it so much too.'

'Listen,' she mentioned, inserting a key into an old fashioned lock. 'I know you've already had a coffee and I don't want to rob you of your sleep, but why don't you come in for a minute and I'll fix you a cup to fortify you for the ride home?'

'Are you sure?' I asked. 'Not too late? Don't you have to work tomorrow?'

'I'm not fussed about that. Up to you. What about your son?'

'Oh… he's on a sleepover.'

'Lucky Bubba junior.'

She turned the key and ushered me inside. I didn't know what I expected, but her apartment was a revelation. It wasn't large, but not small either. It was spotless, and all the furnishings, rugs and fittings were of the highest quality. There wasn't a thing in it that looked like the mass-produced warehoused world the rest of us inhabited. Nearly everyone else's place was grey and white. There was none of that here. The colours were rich and deep: plum, blueberry, squash, and the pile was deep and the fabric dense. It felt softened, almost womb-like, and no sound intruded from outside. There were real Persian rugs on the floor, a sofa you could laze your life away on, and a profound sense of ease abided throughout. It was perhaps the most comfortable home I had ever been in. Soft music was playing in the next room, and it was my favourite piece too, even if I hadn't heard it in a seeming aeon, Debussy, *La Mer*, the muscular bass notes of the deep current beneath the swirling white caps of the treble.

'It's pretty small,' she said, from the adjoining kitchen, 'but it's home.'

'You kidding? It's the most beautiful place I've ever seen.'

'You don't have to say that Bubba. And have you maybe remembered your real name yet? Bubba's nice, but it does sound a little odd for a… grown man.'

This time I didn't need to think. 'Stu,' I said.

'Stu…' she responded, then laughed. 'Well, I've always liked a good stew.'

I chuckled appropriately. But my thoughts were already elsewhere. 'Where do you find great stuff like this? Real wooden furniture, a beatnik coffee table… and this golden cone standing lamp…'

'I like to browse thrift stores. On my days off.'

Thrift stores. I had forgotten all about thrift stores too. How much else had I forgotten?

'Where do you find them, thrift stores?'

'Around. I'll take you if you like.'

'I would. Very much.'

'You know,' she called, 'you don't really seem very much like an insurance man.'

'No?' I toyed with a silk tassel of a rug. 'What do I seem like? And where did you find these rugs?'

'Thrift stores. No-one looks these days. You find everything. And as for your job, I'd say something more to do with ideas.'

'Ideas? What kind?'

She walked into the living room carrying a tray. She had changed into a black kimono, with what looked like the gold embroidered slippers of a pasha on her feet. She seemed to have removed most of her make-up, and only a little mascara and lipstick were left. Mind you, perhaps that's all she ever wore, I wasn't sure. With skin like hers, who needed cosmetics? She set the tray down and I saw there were two mugs of coffee fragrant with cardamom, and two tiny antique crystal glasses with a decanter of spirits.

'Cognac,' she said.

'Oh, I love cognac.'

'Who in their right mind doesn't?'

She sat down beside me, kicked off the slippers and relaxed barefoot. She handed me my coffee. 'Black.'

'And for you too?'

'Yes. Black. I love black. Black is the new black.'

I wanted to tell her I loved her, and only just stopped myself. Could it be possible I'd only met her today?

She poured two glasses of cognac, handed me one and sipped from the other.

'I prefer Spanish cognac,' she said. 'I enjoy its roughness. French is too refined. Like the French.'

'You were saying… what kind of ideas?'

'I don't know. I know insurance must be interesting. But you're so clever. I can tell.'

A little bell tinkled in the back of my mind. Was it, I wondered, that her fiancé… Jed… was doing something brilliant on Mars? Should I ask? I didn't want to, yet I didn't know if I could resist it either. There was so much I needed to know about her.

'Oh,' she said, 'something just for fun now.' She jumped up and slipped out of the room, and a moment later came back in with something else on a tray. She set it down on the carpet, sat down beside me again and crossed her legs. 'It's a made-up version of the model kit you bought for Bubba, like you saw in the store window. ElonGate.'

It was ElonGate all right. The little grid of low, white structures surrounded by plant and equipment, and the rocky red wastes stretching away, the ever-familiar sight everyone on Earth knew from all the photographs and videos. In the distance was the spaceport, studded with tall white ships, and the model of the whole settlement was set in its protective little valley of low hills. In all it was a child's delight.

'I bought one for my nephew,' she said. 'But it turned out he already had one. So one dull evening I sat here and put it all together. It was fun. And look, there are little figures with it too.'

'Where?' I asked, peering forward. Then outside one of buildings, I made out a group in space suits. As my eyes adjusted, I saw more little figures, dotted at work around the settlement.

She was so close to me now I could smell the sweet cognac on her breath, and she touched my arm as the forefinger of her other hand singled out one of the tiny figures.

'See this one? Lying on a stretcher on the ground? Funny, know who he looks like?'

I smiled. 'How could I? It's so tiny.'

'Look a bit closer.'

I did so. 'It's just a plastic little figure with a helmet on.'

'Look extra closely at the face. Try.'

I saw it was a man's face, middle-aged. That's all I could see at first. But as my eyes adjusted further to the minute detailing, I did see more.

'Well...' I remarked, 'amazingly enough he seems to look a little bit... like me.'

'I noticed that too,' she smiled.

'But... I mean, how... that's ridiculous...'

'Now look at the figure bending over him.'

Her nearness now, the contours of her body in contact with mine, her warmth and scent were intoxicating. I felt a little faint, as if they could overwhelm me. It must be the wine, the cognac, or something. Could a woman really have such a presence that you could die in it without a care?

'Look. Please, Stu.'

I moved my face so close to the model my nose was almost touching the tiny figurine. 'Well, and that... looks a bit like you.'

'That's what I thought too,' she nodded. 'Interesting isn't it? Now kiss me, please.'

I needed no further invitation. Her lips had all sweetness of ripe berries, luscious and soft, how I needed them to be soft, and firm, how I needed them to be firm. Then I felt like I'd been kicked in the head by a mule. I saw stars, literally, and the blackness of space fell like a stage curtain.

When my vision returned, my head was on a soft pillow and sunlight was coming in through the window. Her face was near and her eyes were looking deeply into mine, and she was smiling.

'Good morning,' she said.

'Oh... yes,' I said. 'Good morning.'

It was wonderful to see her in the light. She was if anything even more lovely. But an odd thing was that I seemed to be looking up at her, her head was not on a pillow beside me, rather seemingly suspended in the air above me. It was very strange and I tried my best to work it out. I realised then the room was all white, and she was all in white, white as her smile.

'Dr James,' she said.

'Pardon? Who?'

'You are Doctor James. That's your name.'

'No, I'm not... I'm... I'm...'

'And I am a doctor. And you are my patient. And I am so very glad to see you back here, present with me today.'

'What?' I tried to sit up, but she gently restrained me with her palm. 'Where... am I?'

'In hospital in ElonGate. You've been here for weeks, receiving treatment.'

'Treatment? For what?'

'You nearly died in a dust storm, out in the field. And afterwards, you seem to have had some kind of breakdown. We're not quite sure how to describe it yet. But we're slowly getting an idea.' She stopped. 'After the accident, in which your brain was deprived of oxygen for some time, it seems to have gone into shock, and retreated into your past back on Earth. Places you used to know as a young man, a boy, especially a department store, called...'

'Benson Brothers...' I murmured.

'And you seem to have involved me, as your primary therapist, in these memories... tangled up in all kinds of things you've been speaking of for some weeks now... old Hollywood films your grandparents used to show you... places you knew as a child and young man... your father's job... your parents' first meeting and date... even the nickname they gave you as a boy... Bubba... before they died in an accident, and you suffered the trauma of loss, when you were...'

I searched but knew. 'Thirteen.'

'That's right,' she said, with deep relief in her professional voice. 'We of course don't know all about where you've gone in your thoughts, and all you've seen, except what we've heard you say during your sessions... especially things you've said to me. But the good thing is you're back with us again now, at last.' I looked up at her in a halo of sunlight, a golden-haired cherub by an Italian master. 'You should rest now,' she said gently.

'You've got some catching up to do.'

'And... but...,' I searched, '...oh... but what of Masha, Masha... my... wife...'

Her eyes lit up that I remembered, but then dimmed with what she knew she must tell me. 'Sadly, Masha didn't survive the storm. Please accept my sincere and heartfelt condolences,' she said, with a squeeze of my hand.

'Thank you,' I got out. It sounded little more than a whisper.

'Rest now please. I'll be back later. And a counsellor will be calling on you too.'

I was frozen, unable even to look, to think, even to swallow. Masha. My Masha. An eternity seemed to tick by and still the woman I'd known as Ali was above me, seemingly waiting for me to say something. But nothing came, nor could.

She turned to leave. But I didn't want her to go. If she did I would be completely alone, in a world without Masha. Which was then no longer a world, just a place I existed.

'Please, Ali,' I said.

'Yes, Dr James?'

The name sounded hollow. Could that really be me?

'What is your surname?' I asked.

'June. I'm Dr June.'

She stood there near the bed, still, and I knew if I spoke no more, she would have little choice but to go. I cast around for something to say in reply. Any words. Anything.

'What is your first name?'

'Allyson,' she said, smiling gently down at me.

'And... mine? I still can't quite recall it...'

'You will. In time.'

'No. Tell me now. Please. I need you to.'

'Very well then. What else could it be, but Stewart?'

Yellow

He insisted. She didn't mind. She liked it herself. So many shades –
navy, sky, electric, dusky, turquoise, cornflower, periwinkle, ultramarine,
midnight, IKB, and on and on. She did have "shades of opinion", but in the
end liked them all. So here she was in the store, doing it the old-fashioned
way because he had wanted her to go and check things out herself.

The place felt crowded, more than she had expected. Were people
really returning to stores? Was it like vinyl records? The assistant was
an old rooster in an ill-fitting collar and a striped necktie, with sly little
eyes that saw.

'So madam is thinking of drapes, carpet, wallpaper, all in blue?'

'Yes.'

'We do get a few of these. And what will be the function of the room?'

'A special room just for the two of us,' she said.

'So we'll be needing to pick out blue bed linen too.'

With that he did his small fowl smile and she wondered if the drum-
stick would come away easily from the carcass.

The yellow powder was over everything. It was so fine you weren't even
sure it was there, but if she moved she could see a cloud of it stirred up,
smell its rancid yellowness and taste its yellow grit. She saw the granules on the drapes and lamp shades, a film of it on the mantelpiece and
windowsill. It was everywhere. It had to be. She hated yellow unless it was
a lemon, just as she didn't like orange unless it was an orange. Lime she
didn't mind. Yellow was poison and the sun. She sat on the sofa drinking beer and chafing at the dust. She'd been hard at it all day and didn't
feel like she'd be stopping any time soon. She could drink for a month.
Two. Who or what was there to stop her? There was a ten pin of empty

cans on the coffee table and she was weighing up a full one in her hand for a strike. She thought about Loretta. Good drinking company, but she always brought tequila and that never ended well. She once asked how she got a name like that, and Loretta shrugged. She wondered how the hell she was getting on. Loretta drank too much. She herself drank too much too. They all did. What was drink for if not too much? Moderation was a dumb long boring word, the shit of therapists. Loretta always said she was amazed she could drink so much beer and stay trim. The gym and little food helped, but still she knew she was lucky. Loretta had put on a pound or three, not that it would matter much. Their men were on the trip home, almost as long as a pregnancy, and would come back famished for a flesh and blood woman. She was pretty hungry herself. The two of them would eat steak, a lot of it. He loved it, fuck the cost. She popped the can. The robots did the mining. And there were robots to maintain the robots. And so on. But at the end of the chain there still had to be a human. And he was that. Well, after their first day or two in bed he was anyway.

As she sipped her beer she saw something out of the corner of her eye. One of the dust granules moved, or seemed to. It was on the armrest of the sofa. She peered at it closely, microscopically, her eyeball screwed right down onto it. She wondered if it was her imagination, or if she was at last finally, properly drunk. Or if it had really moved. Or was even there. Yellow. Sulphur. Bile, even if they said it was green it had to be yellow. Just as with where it had come from, the dust was really orange-red, but her eyes saw it as yellow. Why, she didn't know. She hated the dust and the yellow was all she saw. Sulphurous yellow. Poisonous yellow. Toadstool yellow. Sometimes she felt trapped in a story she had read in her teens, *The Yellow Wall Paper*. Well, theirs would be blue, blue, blue.

The thing was, if that granule really had moved, then last time he must have brought back something, despite all the endless ablutions and scans, precautions and all the rest, and now it sat, on the arm of her sofa. A granular fucking little Martian. She watched ever more closely. Nothing happened. Maybe it was asleep now, or playing dead, or was dead.

Or wasn't there. She belched, masturbated. One made her feel a bit more comfortable, the other left her feeling kinda OK. Some women resorted to gigolos – oh Lord, how she loved that word, jig-a-jig-a-lo-bro – dildos or tech. She didn't bother. The dust made her feel dirty enough. If she wanted to feel how they did she could go outside and roll naked in the mud, dead drunk like she had on Loretta's tequila. She masturbated again and it quite tired her out. The beer, uh.

She drew back her arm and flung a new full can hard at the ten pins. Most scattered, flying into the window, the armchair, the rugs, showering the room with the stale beer left over in the bottom of the cans. She liked the smell. It reminded her of him. The last pin tottered, but stood. No strike. She cracked another can with one hand and slugged it. She could drink like this for two months, three. What was there to stop her?

She applied the wallpaper with great care. The pattern was *The Great Wave off Kanagawa*, She was a bit concerned about how a whole wall of it might look. Busy as fuck? The other walls were already done: Monet's *Water Lilies*; *Abstraction Blue*, O'Keefe; and a giant *Blue Monochrome*, Klein. She really hoped it wasn't all too much but suspected it was, way. All she hoped was he'd be happy. The sly rooster had somehow sold her on the different art walls idea. He'd tried hard with *Blue Poles*. 'He'll really go for that one.' Quick fowl wink.

The carpet was down. Plain midnight blue at least. But the ceiling was Van Gogh's *Starry Night*. She lay on the bed and looked up... oh god, no, no, it was all too much. Mind you, with the kind of man he was, she'd be the one doing the looking at it most. The sheets, pillow cases and quilt were all cobalt silk. She made the bed carefully, caringly, and when she was finished she looked around the room. It was oceanic, a blue womb, a room just for them. He would fuck her so hard and so gently here, rocking her to sleep like lapping waves as he did at the end, and in the morning she would wake him and get him do it some more, and that was how their days would pass, abandoned to the sweet seas with not a grain of yellow.

The Baroness

It had taken months of negotiations with her agent, and just when he had all but given up hope it had come through. As he went through the front gate he could barely wipe away his grin. The setting was so typically charming, too: a little Cornish cottage in the mist, with the pot-pourri front garden and path leading up to the door. Had not Betjeman himself breathed his last in a Cornish village? There were leadlights in the windows, the ivy creeping up the walls to the thatched roof and, somehow, here he was on the doorstep.

He knocked. Nothing. Knocked again. He heard shuffling inside and at last a woman of about seventy, sharp of eye and nose, opened the door in a ragged tee-shirt, pyjama pants and blue men's slippers, grey hair in stringy strands on her damp brow. She just stood and looked at him. He felt inspected as if by a leery hillbilly.

'I'm Uhuru Ngugi.'

'Are you now?'

He shifted a little on the welcome mat. 'I have an appointment. With the baroness.'

'Her ladyship didn't mention anything. What do you want? The last person who washed up here looking smarty pants as you tried to get in with a fucking *Watchtower*. Mind you, I got him to do the housework while he preached his horseshit. Useful idiot.'

'Queenie?' A woman's voice called behind her. 'What's going on?'

'Some young black chappie at the door,' the woman called back. 'Trying to sell us Jehovah.'

'Why do you mention he's black?' the voice called. 'Getting racist in your old age dear?'

'He's black because he fucking is! It's just a fact.'

'Would you say there's a young white chappie at the door?' the voice yelled.

'Spare me your bourgeois fucking correctness!' she yelled back.

He called past her, 'I'm Uhuru Ngugi! We have an appointment, baroness!'

Queenie gave him a stern looking up and down and hissed. 'Piss off, god nut.'

Another face materialised in the gloom, a woman of similar height and age, but very slight, bony in the shoulders, with a spittle of remnant brown in her cropped hair and the pixie face and gold-rimmed spectacles he knew so well.

'Queenie,' she said patiently, 'I told you Mr Ngugi was coming. He's not from the *Watchtower*. He's from a much more august organ.'

'Oh? And what would that be?'

'*The Guardian*,' he said.

'*The Guardian!!??*' Queenie cried, full bore Lady Bracknell, and scowling ever more suspiciously up at him.

'Queenie, stand back, stand aside please, and let the gentleman in. Come in, Mr Ngugi.' Still eyeballing him, Queenie stepped back a pace and he was able to enter the cottage where Brenda Webster awaited with her trademark quarter-strength smile.

'Baroness,' he said, extending his hand.

She shook it peremptorily. 'Call me Brenda.'

'Yes. Because you do know, don't you,' Queenie put in, with a bony jab of forefinger at his chest, 'that this is *the* Brenda Webster, herself, standing before you? You do know who she is and what she's done I hope, angry young man from *The Guardian*. You'd better. She's the Poet bloody Laureate. Mate.'

'Queenie,' the baroness sighed. 'I'm sure Mr Ngugi is fully prepared. That's why he's come all the way down from London to see me. Now would you please go and make us a pot of tea.' She turned to him. 'Tea do for you, Mr Ngugi? Or coffee, or would you perhaps take a sherry?'

'Tea, thank you. Brenda.' It didn't feel at all right to him to call her that.

'Milk? Sugar? You look the sugar type to me,' Queenie said.

'Just black, thank you.'

Queenie grunted something and walked off.

'And I'll have a scotch while you're at it dear,' the baroness called after her, and waved her hand to him and led him away through a place so dark he could barely even make out the shapes of the furnishings and worried he might knock over something priceless. He wondered why the elderly so often seemed to live in dark houses, then remembered the baroness had a condition of some sort that meant her eyes were hyper-sensitive to light. He'd have to give the readers some idea about the place though, and wondered if he could ask for a lamp or two to be switched on at some point.

He followed her into what he presumed to be her office. She shut the door and sat in a leather chair on the far side of an old wooden desk – nothing special, but he knew he should ask about its provenance – that was surprisingly clear of clutter, nothing like the cliché poet's messy desk. There was a small green notebook with a fountain pen beside it, a Lamy he saw. Fountain pen recidivist she may be, but there was also a laptop open on one side of the desk and, beside it, an Olivetti portable typewriter seemingly in working condition. He wondered if she went pen to type-writer to screen. Lucian Freud on one wall, Bacon on the other – both modest enough pieces but presumably gifted by an admirer of means – and an enormous framed black and white photograph of Ginsberg in full flight at his famous first reading of *Howl* at Six Gallery. One might have known the books on the shelves that backed her: Plath, Bishop, Dickinson, Heaney, Eliot, Auden. If he'd spied *Atlas Shrugged* it would have been news.

'Sit down please, Mr Ngugi.' Her voice had always reminded him of the long-lamented Dame Judi's after enough double somethings and a pack of cigarettes. In person it was even more so, chill and wry. And despite her telling him to address her by her first name, he found himself still mentally calling her "baroness".

He located a chair, pulled it up to the desk and took out a recorder, with his phone as backup and a tablet with his questions, also a second backup. She waited patiently, saying nothing. When he was finished preparing, he looked up into eyes grey as the pelt of a wolf.

'So, Mr Ngugi.. any relation to James Ngugi? Ngugi wa Thiong'o?'

'Distant.'

'"Disdaining nature, pissing poison on it… murmuring gratitude for our shares in the gods of capital…" And I love his *A Grain of Wheat*. What a novel.'

'My grandmother dined with him once in Nairobi. It was a big group dinner. Meja Mwangi was there too.'

'Ah, yes. *Going Down River Road… The Cockroach Dance…* also very fine. Two of Africa's best. Mind you, so many since, so good.' She stopped, murmured 'Africa.'

'Have you been?' he asked.

'Only in my bones. Humanity was born on your continent of course, Mr Ngugi.'

'Call me Uhuru, please.'

'I use formal names for all interviewers. It's better that way. And if it wasn't for Africa, we wouldn't have Homo sapiens, and have all we do as a species. With all the Earth ours. And Mars too. Funny, I've been to Mars, but not Africa.'

Queenie walked in without knocking, sloshed a mug of tea down in front of him and handed the baroness a tumbler of scotch.

'Thank you,' he said. The baroness nodded and Queenie left with a deep ironic bow and tug of forelock.

'So, are you writing a novel Mr Ngugi? Every journalist of any worth is. It's a shit job with a French name.'

He took a moment. 'Yes, I am.'

'What about?'

'Well, I'm not really sure yet.'

'How far in?'

'Seventy or so thousand words, first draft.'

'Good. That you don't know yet. A good novel is not a planned birth. It's a love child.' She sipped her scotch. He took a little tea and got a mouthful of leaves. 'Queenie's a good egg but she can't make tea to save her life. Life's too short for tea anyway.' She took the mug from him, opened the window and dumped it out, tipped half her scotch into the mug and handed it back to him. 'Cheers,' she said, and they raised cups, clanked and drank.

'Nice drop,' he said.

'Well come on then Mr Ngugi. Let's get to it.'

'May I start recording?'

'Of course.'

He touched buttons and got all three recordings going, and she started up without a question. 'You're here to find out how I spent nearly a year on Mars on the public purse, and despite being some fancy poet haven't published a single line about it. And don't try to deny that's what it is. I've turned down dozens who wanted the same thing. What else would you be here for?' She looked at him and he didn't deny it. 'My commission, which I was honoured to receive, was to write about the experience of being on Mars. Simple as that. Though I think the committee secretly hoped I'd come back with my own *Odyssey*. But of course they haven't been there, to Mars.' She took a smidge of whisky. 'In my first month at ElonGate I felt like a caged rat in a lab. Confined, claustrophobic, dank. That's about how pleasant it is. The only thing that makes it tolerable living there is knowing everyone is part of history. And the Mess bar.'

'A lot of people say it's difficult.'

'Human beings cut off from all their connections back on Earth. Many fearing they might never get back to those they love. What else could it be? Endless talk about radiation too. The perils of just venturing outside. The corrosion of sanity within the four small walls of your domus. You hear everything, the living spaces are cramped, walls thin. People screaming, fighting, fucking, coughing, laughing, singing, farting, weeping. It's all around you. And no way out. Let's put it this way, you can't just step out for a breath of air.'

She swilled the rest of her scotch, unlocked the desk drawer and pulled out a bottle. 'Don't tell Queenie. She thinks I'm rotting my liver.

Mind you, she's got a stash and her own rotting liver too.' She held up the bottle, he nodded and she topped up his glass. 'Drinking on the job. Good, Mr Ngugi.'

'So you left.'

'No choice. If I'd stayed there, I thought, I'd end up writing doggerel.' He smiled at that, and she gave him a look that said she couldn't be flattered. 'It took time of course.' She peered up into the tall shadows where the cobwebs crept. 'I met a young man over beers in the Mess. Horny little chap. A pocket devil. And that's all I'll say on that topic.'

He took a sip. 'And this is a nice scotch too, thank you.'

'Civilisation must endure, even in deepest Cornwall.'

They drank on in silence as Queenie began coughing convulsively in the next room. She hacked and hacked. It sounded like a life and death struggle with phlegm.

'Is she all right?' he asked.

'As my doctor once said to me when I was ill, you'll either get better or die. Queenie smokes on the sly as well as drinks. Her clothes stink worse than a knackery.'

While they waited for Queenie to splutter herself into quiet or death, he took the opportunity to run his eyes a little more searchingly over the bookshelves. On closer inspection a few were almost surprising. *Notes from the Underground* sat beside Sitwell's *Façade*. Next to that was *The Female Eunuch*, Malinowski's *Argonauts of the Western Pacific*, and Reich's *The Mass Psychology of Fascism*. And adjoining them he saw a battered paperback set of the *Illuminatus* trilogy.

'I love *Illuminatus*,' she said, somehow knowing. 'I can't tell you how much silly pleasure I derive from a world that can no longer tell it's fiction.'

'No wonder we had to escape to Mars.'

She almost did her quarter-smile at that. 'So, yes, and as you've already gathered, I soon chafed at being stuck in ElonGate. I wanted to be on Mars, the real Mars, not in some squalid clutch of bedsits.'

'Surely they arranged excursions.'

'A few laps around the block in those crawling tractor things they have. And after an hour or two we'd be back, and that was my "experience" of Mars. And they'd ask how is the "poetry writing" going, like it was cooking that just needed a pinch of salt. Who could be more alien in a place like ElonGate than a poet? They think we're all impoverished eccentrics. Which we are up to a point, but not how they think. The truly impoverished in this world are all the non-poets. Only they don't know it. Sleepwalking into oblivion, never reflecting even for a moment on what they're doing and where they're going. Inhaling, never exhaling. The soul dies of asphyxiation, and they go on as zombies to their tombs.'

Queenie was at it again. This time the bout went on and on. The baroness didn't budge.

'Shouldn't we…' he said.

'Nothing anyone can do. I've tried for years. She'd secretly smoke underwater.'

Queenie went quiet again, after a final flourish of hacks. He didn't say anything. The baroness looked straight ahead. 'You know who Queenie is of course.'

'I know she was a poet at some point.'

'No. She wasn't a poet, Mr Ngugi. She was a genius of a poet. One of the greatest these blighty isles have ever borne. She was fire and she was majesty. Love in a bud in a couplet. The rain running down your window as your lover gets into the last taxi you'll ever see them in.'

'What happened?'

'You don't know?'

'I tried to research her. Didn't find much.'

'No. It's not easy. Some time ago she paid a tech infant to erase her from the web. Did it pretty well too. She even goes around to actual libraries stealing and burning her collections, anthologies she's in, textbooks with a chapter or passage about her. Some libraries have even marked her as an official menace and banned her on sight.' She was speaking more quickly now. 'In her twenties, people queued for her readings. For a poetry reading, right… not just another stupid gadget. Her books sold. Critics creamed. I was a minor nothing back then, a minnow. I'd go to her readings and take the Tube home in a stupor. Bach might have composed it. Hendrix might have played it. Shakespeare might have written it. But she was it.'

'So what happened?'

'Well. There was a review. More a slag-off of her entire body of work, even her performances, while panning her latest collection as "derivative" of some obscure Russian I know she'd never even heard of.' She stopped, took a steadying breath. 'Queenie had never taken much notice of crits before. But that one she did. It was devastating, ruthless and long. Full page, with pic. Shattered her confidence. The critic went on to an illustrious career as a neo-post-modernist literary Svengali. Queenie fled to a valley in Wales and basically gave up.'

Now she said it, he did recall something. It had all happened a decade before his birth but was still quietly notorious. He reproached himself for not having dug harder. Lazy.

'And the critic wrote for...'

'*The Guardian.*'

'So...' he said, floundering a little now, 'so why... would you agree to me interviewing you.... when I'm from...'

'Because I've read all your work and followed your career as a cultural observer and literary critic, Mr Ngugi. And I knew if I was ever going to speak to anyone about this, it had to be you, no matter where you were from and what Queenie might feel.' She sipped, thought. 'And, well, there are some things we all have to get over in life. Boils lanced to heal.'

He had a terrible intuition. 'I hope Queenie and *The Guardian* is not the real reason you agreed to speak to me.'

'Don't be foolish, because I know you're not.' She held up the bottle. He hesitated, then nodded and she topped up their glasses. He glanced at his phone. Twenty past eleven and onto their third, but the baroness might just have had tea for all it seemed to do to her. 'And that's where I met her, in Wales, in a pub in Cardiff, and we've lived together most of our lives since.' She raised her glass and drank.

'With her a forgotten nonentity... and you now Poet Laureate.'

'Fate. Shit, I know,' she shrugged. 'And so now we may proceed to the nub, Mr Ngugi. I'll pave the way. That horny young devil I met in the Mess, I won't give his name in case of reprisals, even now, worked maintaining those tractor things. And when I told him what I wanted, he told me each one had at least two hand-wheeled "emergency pods" with oxygen, supplies, even a special radiation-proof tent a person can survive in down to minus 80 Celsius. And he copied me with a chart of the emergency shelters sited in an arc around ElonGate. Then, bless his heart, he gave me a contact who got me attached to a research expedition.'

'That much we kind of know, if not the details. But anything more we don't.'

'And that's why you're here, as a gentleman from the gentlefolkery *Guardian*. I always enjoy it, by the way. But it's hard to go past *The Telegraph* for its goat-fucking freemasonry. I relish every encrypted syllable. Who needs *Illuminatus* when you've got *The Telegraph*?'

'So you headed out.'

'With a group of Swedes. We drank some very good stuff on the way. I told them my one word of Swedish: *Systembolaget*… government grog shop. A fine crew, those Swedes. They even played Abba and we danced around the cabin as we crawled along for hours, slept the night and ventured on. We passed mountains, gorges, traversed endless rocky plains and desolation so obsidian it seared the eye with its perfect hardness,' she said. 'And the next day, as they all went off with their science stuff, I said I was staying behind to write about what I'd seen so far, and then took one of the wheeled pods, stepped out in my suit, switched off communications and transponders and so on as the horny young devil had shown me, and strode off in the opposite direction, dragging the pod and whistling *Waterloo*. To pillage Dr King, free, free, free at last.'

'Did you know where you were going? Were you trying to get anywhere?'

'No. Beyond an emergency shelter, in my own time. I knew I couldn't go to the closest one as they'd expect that. I was only too aware I had precious little time until some drone or other gismo located me, and so I used it well. I walked. I looked. I walked.'

'What was it like?'

'There is a harshness of a kind I cannot even begin to describe. If you wonder why not one line has come from me, imagine this. That first day I walked to the top of the nearest hill, and standing there as night came, I stood unshielded beneath the stars on an alien world. A sentient creature, not just a life form, but a reasoning entity, alone, under the Milky Way, the universe, whatever it may be.'

She stopped, and for a moment he wondered if that was it.

'Here was *The Waste Land*. A place naked of life, stripped even of atmosphere, in every sense. Yet that atmosphere overwhelmed me. Without life to screw it up, the universe was overwhelming, commanding, brilliant. These orange-red rock-strewn plains of nothing, these mad gargantuan mountains with no-one to stand on them, barren skies that fled before the eye, they were the perfection of creation, untroubled by the messiness of life, and here I had, like a landlady goddess, arrived to view my own little patch. It was pure and exquisite as it was eternal, and for this moment all I surveyed was mine only to see. I drew no conquistador puffed-chestedness at that, but did get a modicum of satisfaction that it was me, a poet, not a boffin, surveyor or engineer, who had first laid a close human eye upon every pebble I beheld.'

She stopped again and he found the time to recall that here he was, in a gloomy Cornish cottage where most people would bang their head on the lintels, listening to someone slip off alone into the wastes of Mars. And for what... poetry? That was all very fine. But worth her life?

'Did you ever think you were taking an unnecessary risk?'

'No. Yes. But then I wasn't Plath, gassing myself over that crow Ted Hughes... or Shelley drowning while "pleasure-boating" in a wild storm. I was doing something no human had ever done before. Yes I was gambling absurdly with my life, but I had no dependants or family, well, other than Queenie, so I could at least try to have something akin to a genuine experience of this other world, and, from the thoughts and emotions it provoked in me, perhaps sprinkle a pinch of poetic pixie dust back on my own human race.'

'How far did you get?'

'Like the hippie Jesus, I was gone two days and nights. Funny how Christians can't even count. Crucified by the Romans on a Friday afternoon – do you remember Hemingway's *Today is Friday* with the two soldiers in the tavern later saying "he did all right up there" or such – and he's dead all Saturday but rises from the dead at sparrows on Sunday morning, dead on my reckoning as little as 36 hours, not 72. The three days stuff is probably more to do with some triple goddess worship or something... did dear old Mr Graves ever mention it, I wonder.' She stopped. 'Oh, sorry. Sorry to be rambling tediously on. It's the only crime.'

He smiled. 'You're not. Go on, please.'

'Well. I kind of froze in the tent for two nights, and somehow got myself to one of the emergency shelters... and when I arrived I must have tripped some e-buzzer or something, and before I knew it there was a drone hovering and staring at me and then one of the tractor things came trundling along. I was apologetic, gave some excuse. I can't even remember what. Nervous attack or something. Got shunted back to ElonGate and put on the next ship out.'

'And here you are back home.'

'Weirdly I felt more at home there. Earth is too dense, cloddy, rotting, rank. Mars is swept clean, seven maids with seven mops. Nothing touches the face of Mars but a little powder. It's tough. Harsh. Glorious. Some might say the glory of God. I just say glory. It's enough.'

'So, you never wrote...'

'How could I? Every word signifies a notion that fails to tell the full truth. And what I experienced there was that... utter truth. We live in a dead universe. Mostly gas. A giant celestial fart. A few flecks of fire in it, like a kid's held a lighter to the Cosmic Arse. It's chemistry, not biology. Physics, not philosophy. Tougher than Nietzsche, more pointless than Camus.' She looked him in the eye. 'It's perfection unto itself. And so, accordingly, Mr Ngugi, I wrote nothing. Because no word is ever perfect for meaning, and so it is perfect not to write it.'

He was about to attempt a rejoinder when Queenie barged in and tossed something into his lap. 'There it is!! You wanted it!! That's it! Now fuck the right off!'

The thing in his lap looked like an old-fashioned typed manuscript. The cover page read "ElonGate: Poems by Brenda Webster".

'Queenie!! You fucking bitch hag!!' the baroness yelled, leaping to her feet.

'That's it!' Queenie roared at me. 'That's what she wrote! It's a lie! She wrote it all right. She wrote and wrote! But now she hates it and lies about it! "Not good enough for what I felt," she says... And it's beautiful! *Beautiful!* Take it and read it and give it to her fucking publisher and let me out of my misery here!'

The baroness leapt and went for it but Queenie was surprisingly quick, grabbed her hand and the next thing they were arm-wrestling and on the floor, fighting.

'You old harridan!'

'You witch! Utter witch!!!' Queenie screamed. 'I edited that book! Every bloody word!! Pound to your pathetic Eliot! More! I wrote half of it!!'

'Yeah?? I didn't see you on fucking Mars!!'

'I didn't need to go to fucking Mars!' Queenie yelled. 'At least you did that much!'

He jumped to his feet. 'Ladies, please!' It sounded stupid even to his own ears.

They rolled over and over on the floor, knocking down a lamp and a chair.

'Get out!' Queenie screamed at him. 'Go back to your fucking *Guardian* and write all this shit up!'

'Yes! Go!' the Baroness yelled at him. 'You got what you wanted! Take it and get the fuck out of here! Burn it!!'

'No!! Don't!!' Queenie roared.

He rustled his things together as they wrestled and spat and scratched, then stumbled away through the darkened house. He stepped out into the open air on the welcome mat, saw it was raining, put the manuscript under his jacket and ran to his car.

Late that night as his wife slept beside him, he took out the manuscript. He wondered if it was the only copy. For such a fuss it had to be, he guessed. He started reading. As he put it down and switched out the bedside lamp just before dawn, he thought that in the film version he would have burnt it, or gone out in the morning mist down to the Thames in his dressing gown and slippers, and tossed it into the river. In the film version he would have deleted his interview recordings too.

When he awoke a few hours later he took a cab and delivered the manuscript to Brenda Webster's publisher. It was of course dazzling, groundbreaking, literally. But there were some cadences he couldn't shake the strange feeling may be Queenie's. Pound to her Eliot… or something else possibly?

On the way back home a call came in from her agent. He ignored it. He ate a plate of bacon and eggs in the kitchen and his wife smiled, presumably to see him with an appetite. She always said he worked too hard and ate too little. He rang his editor and said he needed to mull on the story for a while, and she said no rush. He also said there might be another development with it and left it at that. He went on to say he was thinking of taking some time off to visit his family in Nairobi. When he asked his wife she smiled and said "yes let's go". She knew him well enough to leave it at that.

The Last Night on Earth

We sat in a splodge of yellow light in a corner of the near-empty diner. 'Look, we're in our own little bubble of Hopper,' I said.

'Nice,' Jess said. She loved Hopper, but tonight was a different night. 'He painted perfect loneliness,' she added.

'Will you be wanting anything more?' the sole waitress rasped. I nodded for the check and she walked off. We got up and I helped Jess into her jacket. 'Quite the gentleman aren't we,' the waitress said, returning with the check and an exaggerated wink for Jess, who managed to smile back.

The windswept street was cold and felt like an abandoned car park. With the malls strangling the last of downtown, in a way it was. It might feel right to be leaving, if we were going together. We walked through brittle shadows. The streets aren't mean, but they aren't kind either. Her hand rested with mine and I felt reassurance grow from the heart of her palm and warm me through. But I knew I would soon be cold.

'Maybe it won't be anything like as bad as they say.'

'I doubt it,' she said.

'But it doesn't seem possible.'

'Why not?'

'They did so much research. Took every measure.'

'Uh-huh.'

'What do you mean?'

'It's a virtual epidemic,' she said. 'People can't take it up there. Why do you think they need to send so many people like me? People can't deal with it there and the people in charge can't deal with all the people who can't deal with it there. So they're shipping in legions of psychs.'

A passing bus muted talk. I realised she was navigating me in the direction of her apartment. 'I thought you'd packed it all up now.'

'The bed's still there. Last bottle of champagne in the fridge and corn flakes in the kitchen.'

'Perhaps we should get married,' I said.

She glanced over. 'Married? And... what... tonight?'

'Well. Yeah.'

'What, you think there's some drive-in preacher in this town? I mean it's Southern, but not that far down.'

'That's kinda funny,' I said.

'If we were going to do it we should have last week, last month, last year.'

'Why didn't we?'

'I wouldn't know that, Marcus,' she said, a little acid. I hated it when she called me that, instead of stuff like honey and darling. She always meant everything. 'You just wanted to put it off, and to do it now would say to me you don't trust me.'

'For four years.'

'So?'

'You'll meet lots of people,' I said. 'And it's so very far away.'

'No kidding. So it's true, you really don't trust me. And you'll meet people too.'

'But Jess, you know I'd never even think of...'

'But you think I fucking might??'

'I do trust you. But it's four fucking years!'

'So you expect me to trust you even though you don't seem to trust me. And you think some stupid vow might somehow fix that?'

'No,' I said. 'Especially if you think it's stupid. But I do think it affirms who we are. Together. As a married couple you can say "Mrs" if you want to.'

'Instead of doctor?'

'Of course not. But you'd have a, you know, ring on your finger, and someone might say something and you could say well, yes, I'm married. I'm a Mrs as well as a doctor.'

'Uh-huh. OK then.' She thought a moment, mid-stride. 'So if that's what you mean... maybe we could do a *Breakfast at Tiffany's*.'

'How do you mean?'

'They got a wedding ring from a Cracker Jack box. And got it engraved from that nice kind gentleman behind the counter at Tiffany's.'

'I can only ever remember you talking about your diagnosis of Holly's borderline personality disorder. Which I thought was nothing more than her wanting to marry a rich guy so she didn't have to take 50 bucks for the "Powder Room" and sleep with random creeps any more. But then I did think you might be a bit right when she dumped poor Cat out of the taxi in the rain. That showed a pretty twisted bent.'

'Hey,' she said. 'There's that joke store up ahead. I think it's still open.'

'You mean not boarded up.'

'I mean still open for business at this time of night.'

'So?'

'So we can buy our wedding rings from the joke store.'

'You're, er, joking, right?'

'Nope. And the counter clerk can marry us.'

'Jess. They're not the captain of a ship.'

'No. But it is a crucial piece of urban infrastructure.'

'They'd need a weird sense of humour.'

'Who else works in a joke shop?'

Bill's Corner Joke Store was a smoky glazed, half-lit, muddled and fuddled Hades of rubber horror masks, Halloween wigs, broomsticks, hand buzzers and whoopee cushions. In recent years it had moved more into movie and gaming franchise merch, from boxed toys and games to the costumes and replica weaponry fans craved like the golden apples of the sun. The store was the kind of place that should legally be frequented only by boys under the age of ten, but more often than not was the habitual hang of pudgy 40-year-olds in Star Wars T-shirts looking for their cosplay *piece de resistance* at a Vintage Comicon. Dust, grime and must are obligatory in this kind of joint, as is the kooky lone counter attendant, who in this case looked the full Mad Magazine kid, Alfred E. Neuman, the illegitimate spawn of Woody Allen and R. Crumb. He was perfectly scrawny, geeky and weird, and so very inevitably here.

'How old are you?' Jess asked, walking straight up to the counter.

'What? Why?'

'Are you over eighteen?'

'Who the hell are you? Cops looking for some porn shit to stick?'

'No,' I said, 'we want you to marry us.'

He stared at us through his regulation bottle-bottom glasses, so thick and greenish you could see a little Sargasso weed adrift in there. 'What the hell? You think I'd want some kinda … fuckin' thrupple with you two?'

'Maybe you would,' Jess went on, in her "fuck you're an idiot" quiet tone now, in which I never failed to hear cadences of the clinician. 'But in this instance we just want you to officiate at our marriage here tonight.'

'Oh… whoa… yeah!' cheered a stringy, hillbilly-bearded Trekkie, emerging from behind an ancient flaking cardboard life-sized Chewbacca. More bizarros began to appear, as if from thin air or parallel universes, but presumably from some secret "Whacko Members Only" aisle of the store.

'You want me to pronounce you two man and wife?' the assistant said, grasping it now in all its nutty significance.

'We do,' we chorused perfectly, looked at each other in surprise and mouthed "snap".

He gave it a little thought. 'Well, I mean it's a pretend wedding, right… won't count. You want it for the theatre of the, like, absurd of it, or what the hell ever.'

'Kinda,' I said. 'It'll mean a whole lot more than that to us, but you're at least in the ballpark. What's your name?'

'Waldo. And don't say anything I haven't heard about that, OK.'

'All right, Waldo,' I said. 'And just for the record, how old are you?'

'I'm 27 man.'

'Yeah? Well keep talking whatever you are.'

There was a laugh at that, and we became aware a little group was starting to congregate around us like zombies from the night, balding men with pot bellies in raggedy old Frank Zappa T-shirts, and pallid, near transparent, fish-eyed teen women in Harry Potter hoodies who looked like they only ever left a computer to shit or come here, and mad, bespectacled hunters and hoarders of original, cellophane-wrapped boxed toy figures.

'So what do you say, Waldo? Think of it as gift wrapping for the rings we're going to buy,' Jess said. 'I hope you've got rings.'

'Oh yeah, rings we got, totally. Star Wars, Jack Sparrow, Dementors, Captain America, or just your regular skull and crossbones, squirt rings, fart stink rings... we've got 'em all.'

The little crowd started pressing in a bit closer now, and few appeared to have washed for a while and I was starting to get a bit of a *Day of the Locust* thing, wondering if we shouldn't just forget it and get back to Jess's place and make out while we still could. But like a competent stage magician Waldo, with a flourish of sorts, produced a black velvet tray of trinkets, and Jess pored over them.

'Come on then darling,' she said to me, 'come and choose.'

'Would you like matched ones?' Waldo asked professionally. 'I mean, you could have a Bellatrix Lestrange gothic bird's head ring for the bride, and a blue-fire Dumbledore opal for the groom. That dude has the coolest rings. And these are, like, uber-rare. Not cheap though,' he added, looking up at me and making me wonder if these people all dug horror so much they never went to the dentist.

'I want Bellatrix to bear my ten Death Eater sons,' a hunched overcoat at the back said, and was jumped on with 'Sexist Slytherin pig!!' by a matching pair of identikit Goths in Hermione Granger hoodies.

Waldo produced the Bellatrix ring from a drawer beneath the counter and gave it to Jess. 'I'm gonna go Cinderella on this,' she said. 'If the ring fits, wear it.' She tried it on and it did.

'Oh, oh...' one of the Hermiones protested, 'but that's a, like, total misreading of the fairy tale. It's not her who needs it to fit.'

'Totally,' affirmed a zoned-out Trekkie through a cumulus of weed breath. 'It's the prince dude that's looking for the...'

'Perfect fit,' the Hermione giggled, and he laughed pottily with her.

I wondered, could there possibly be a double hitching in the Haunted House tonight?

I noticed one ring that might in some respects be just a bit elegant: two rotating orbs of blue stone in what looked like a flattened sine wave mesh of silver. 'What about this one?'

'*Ooh...* I like that,' Jess said.

'That's the Princess Leia ring from *The Last Jedi!*' ejaculated a "Guaranteed Original Star Wars Luke Skywalker" branded T-shirt, and the rest of the zombies almost swooned. I was starting to feel like we were trapped in the actual Star Wars bar scene. The original of so, so many similar ones in the old franchise shit my younger siblings had made me watch.

Jess liked it and tried it on, and that one fitted too. 'Nice,' she said, holding up her hand for me, 'what do you think?'

'Better than from a Cracker Jack box,' I said.

'Hey... I love Cracker Jack,' Hermione said, hurt. 'Don't gaslight me, man.'

'Sorry, not my intention,' I said. 'And I'm sure you do love your Cracker Jack too.'

'And, hey, I happen to have this totally cool Darth Vader one that could go with it,' Waldo enthused.

'Oh, man!!' one of the zombies yelled, 'no-one can fuckin' get them!!'

'You obviously don't know your Star Fleet Admiral Waldo well enough,' he grinned, and I couldn't help but notice one ear went a bit lower than the other as he did.

He rummaged in a drawer and pulled out a tiny black velvet bag, and in it was a ring fashioned from a black Darth Vader helmet.

'*Oh, whoa... that's iconic!*' a zombie yelled.

'So...' Jess gave me a coquettish little smile, 'how about if I get the Princess Leia... and you get the Darth? Though we could do a cool gender reversal on that, too. But I kinda like the blue and silver of the Leia one, so let's stick with that.'

'I don't care. You know how much I hate all those dumb movies anyway. But considering where you're going, I guess so, yeah.'

'Hey… hold on…' something pricked Hermione. 'So… where… are you going?' she asked.

'Mars,' Jess said.

'What?? You're fucking, fucking with us, right?' Hermione said.

'No. I'm going to Mars. I head down to Florida tomorrow. We leave in a week or so.'

'You mean you're going to fuckin' ElonGate?' Waldo said. 'You'll be living in ElonGate… I mean… Jesus fuckin' Christ… *ElonGate*.'

The zombies were as hushed as the devout in a cathedral.

'Yes. For a posting of…' and Jess looked at me, 'two years… which with travel, means that's well over three I'm away.'

'Oh… my… God… she's really goin' to fuckin' Mars…' breathed Hermione, and seemed to stagger a little. Her pot-breathed chevalier grasped her and held her safely, looking as if he'd never let go.

'So what will you do doing there… on Mars?' Waldo asked.

'I'm a psychiatrist.'

'Psychiatrist?' he said. 'Who'd need a psychiatrist in ElonGate? I mean, it's on fuckin' Mars, man. It's everyone's dream to even just like see it, y'know.'

'I'd give my left fuckin' ball to go there!' a Trekkie declared.

'Not both?' a gangly transparent woman said, to some laughter.

'Hey, that's totally like cruel,' Hermione 2 said, stepping forward. 'You could harm his mental wellness, bitch.'

'Psychiatric services are needed everywhere,' Jess said calmly, surveying them all. 'Have you ever thought of the isolation there? Not seeing people you love for years except on a screen, and with a long delay? You can't touch, even have a conversation with them. No phone. No immediate chat. None of that. And you might be in a job you've come to hate, with no way to leave it. Or in a bad relationship, with so few options to move on.'

They all went quiet again.

'Don't sound quite so bad to me…' the transparent woman said, though others demurred.

'But... Mars, man... it's fuckin' Mars...' Waldo persisted. 'I love Mars. We all love Mars. Mars is the future. Earth is so fuckin' screwed.'

'Totally,' Hermione 2 muttered, and the others intoned it too. 'Totally.'

We slipped the Princess Leia and Darth rings on each other's fingers. 'I now pronounce you man and wife. Marcus, you may kiss your bride Jessica, and Jessica you may kiss your groom Marcus,' Waldo intoned in his best churchy tone, and when our lips met, the little crowd of zombies went nuts applauding, and they all came up and kissed us and shook our hands and I saw they were all good and nice people and felt guilty I had needed my "learnings" on that, as with so much other shit. Maybe one day Jess might even say I'd "grown".

After we said our goodbyes, I went to pay Waldo for the rings but he said 'Fuck man, for Mars, never. I'll just say they were stolen. Forget it.' And they all waved us off at the door.

I held Jess's hand ever more tightly as we walked away.

'How does it feel to be married?' she said.

'I thought you'd never ask.'

Dark Matter

This was her fourth field trip with Dr McCluskey, checking installations near ElonGate monitoring seismic activity. Mars had far fewer tremors than Earth, but they still occurred, and it was their job to check the instruments and ensure they were all working properly. It had become common practice to team female and male scientists on two-crewed single-day field missions. There were of course larger, longer expeditions with bigger crews, but for short single-day missions gender mixing was considered optimal for mental wellbeing. That wasn't to say there weren't occasional "entanglements" and complications. They'd all banter in the Mess about those, and say the only word they needed to, 'Mars'. Someone would inevitably chime in with '…and Earth', and they'd all laugh.

Her field trips with McCluskey were entirely professional, their conversations confined to work and inconsequential chitchat. It was his turn at the controls, and Linda sat just looking out at all the red dirt. It never ceased to amaze her how utterly empty it was. Geography, nothing more. Its only interest lay in its existential monotony. McCluskey – Mack, inevitably – drove with intent. No-one needed to drive but they all did as it still seemed to give satisfaction, and everyone on Mars found themselves in need of at least some genus of that. Mack wasn't exactly dour, but he wasn't the life of the party either. He had intent in everything he did, right down to the act of breathing, with his deep inhalation and sharp puffs of exhalation.

'Just a whole lot of nothing isn't it,' she said.

'And still no aliens,' he replied, with a hint of a smile, which was something coming from him. 'Where are all the little green men?'

'Underground,' she said, 'with the little green women, just waiting for us to relax… and then zap!'

This time a smile was more discernible on his lips. 'Though in some ways,' he went on, 'it looks a lot like home to me.'

She knew he was Australian, but beyond that wasn't sure what "home" meant for him.

'I'm a West Australian,' he said. 'And Western Australia is half of Australia. Iron oxide… red, red as far as the eye can see. Like Mars. With air.'

She chuckled at that. Was this really McCluskey? She'd never known him to make amusing remarks beyond the odd sarcastic aside over beers in the Mess.

He seemed to read her. 'I know most people here think I'm a bit blah, without much of a sense of humour. But I do have one. I'm Australian, and Australians think we're uniquely gifted on Earth with a sense of humour. Which has always struck me as funny in itself. We also think of ourselves as "laconic". Which is what we call ourselves while we're trying to think of something to say.'

She smiled again and looked over at him. He wasn't a bad looking man, if you were looking for one. He had the "scientist's beard", ginger in his case, to match his casual unruly curls. He was, she supposed, "burly". He certainly did look strong. She had passed him a few times while he was working out in the gym and he never skimped there. She didn't really know if he had ever noticed her as a woman. Not that she would want that. She had her own life. Their circumstances at ElonGate and their relationships back on Earth meant some chose to power down that side of themselves for the duration of their stay. Others inevitably saw it as an opportunity to cut loose, freed literally from Earthly constraints, and the rumour mill was always churning.

He sensed her looking his way. 'What is it?'

'Just looking around. At more nothing.'

'Uh-huh.'

They drove on in silence.

'So Linda, which part of China are you from?

'Well, I'm not from China. I mean, I'm not Chinese, I'm Chinese-American.'

'Yeah I know that,' he said, a little irritation in his voice. 'But where before that?'

'Shanghai. My parents were born there, grew up there, married, and went to America.'

'Doing what?'

'My dad is a doctor and my mum is a college professor.'

'A professor where?'

'Stanford. And yes it's my alma mater. They live in Oakland.'

They drove on through another stretch of silence. The rover was so quiet it was as if they were tucked in the belly of a snake slithering across the sand.

'Chink,' he said.

'Pardon?'

'Chink.'

'What, in armour?'

'No. It's what white Australians used to call Chinese. Australia was a very racist country – still is in some parts. The Chinese arrived early on, thousands of them went to the Victorian goldfields in the 1850s. Some of them were prospectors but others ran the shops that sold the miners picks and shovels, gunpowder, flour and tea, sugar and grog. They stood with them too, at Eureka, a rebellion of the miners against the government over taxes. Australia's only real armed rebellion.'

She had never heard him utter so many words at one time.

'But the Chinese were always seen as "less than white". As late as the 1960s we had a political party leader who said "two wongs don't make a white."'

'Really?'

'His name was Arthur Caldwell, and despite being a progressive immigration minister he agreed with the so-called White Australia Policy, and it wasn't dumped until the 1970s.'

'God.'

'Poor fella my country,' he said.

'Dark Matter,' she found herself saying. 'That's how I view racism. So petty, stupid. So dark. And dark is the binary of light, that gives us life.'

'Dark Matter, the concept, it shits me,' he said. 'Totally fucking shits me'

'Why?'

'Because it's so stupid. We don't know what it really is, or how it works, except by the movement of the tiny percentage of things we can actually see in the universe, the stuff made up of matter. So, with our grand human imagination, we just call the stuff we can't see "Dark Matter". It sounds like something the mediaeval Church would have come up with. "Oh, but what is all this stuff we can't see around us, Holy Father?" "We call it Dark Matter, my son. Now suck my dick and go in peace." It's like a Papal Bull one of the Innocents or Clements might have come up with. Or Alexander VI in his downtime when he wasn't off rooting his little hornbag in the Papal apartments. Yes, well it's bull all right. The very term connotes our failure as the high priests of our own faith of science. We pretend we're getting a handle on how the universe works, with Einstein, Newton and Aristotle as headlights on our benighted road. Yet we find ourselves now peering into a fog of mystery, of "Dark Energy" and "Dark Matter". We don't have a clue what they really are and delude our faithful who follow us like the flock that followed the popes no matter how many choirboys and girls they fucked. Their "Dark Matter" was sin. The underbelly Catholics hide and whisper through the confessional mesh like a cosmic membrane. And if we're frank and honest for just one minute we'd admit our understanding of "Dark Matter" is on a factual par with Biblical Creation. It might as well be it for all we know for sure.'

The length of this peroration from him was quite shocking to her. What was happening to the "laconic Aussie"? But there was something in his tone, and she was not sure why she felt it, that quietly flashed "caution" to her, a warning bell tinkling in the back-brain. She tried to dismiss it: after all, he was only speaking things he clearly felt passionately about, and they were indeed the high priests of a science, which was by definition significantly less than complete in its knowledge and trying to find out more and, he was right, often they experienced deep frustration at their intellectual impotence. The two of them might at this moment be traversing the surface of an alien planet courtesy of the advancements of science, but all around them an unseen world spread away into infinity, or "folded back on itself", or was just one of a multiverse... or whatever.

'But,' he resumed, the cold anger in his tone deepening, 'I'd prefer it if we were fucking honest with ourselves for once and just called it "X" or "Y". I hate the terms, that's all, Dark This and Dark That. I can't even say properly how much I hate it. Dark Matter from the Dark Ages. That's what it fucking is.'

He drove on but ever more agitated, running the rover closer to edges, in fact so close an alarm sounded with a warning of an imminent automatic override. She felt he was doing it to unnerve her. And that thought, even more than his driving, did unnerve her. Yet she also knew that to complain, protest, even caution him in any way would be a mistake and give him what she sensed he wanted from her now. Fear.

'How much further to the monitoring station?' she asked, professional tone.

He looked at her and looked again, and there was something she didn't like in that look at all.

'Can't you see on the fucking screen in front of you? Seven k.'

She nodded and tried not to look at him. Mercifully his eyes returned to the way ahead, possibly on the lookout for something more to alarm her with, and then, by slow degrees, they swivelled back, almost mechanically, her way. She felt his eyes on her, cold blue as a clear winter dusk. 'You hate me.'

She was genuinely surprised. 'What the... Mack? No!'

'I want that suit off you,' he said, looking ahead again. 'I want to see you as you really are. All of you. *Now.*'

'What?'

'I fucking mean it!'

'Are you all right Mack?'

'Oh yeah, call me Mack. Matey Mack. Quiet Macka. My mate Mack. Forget it. I want it off you and now. Down to the fucking skin!'

She couldn't believe her own ears. This must be some kind of sudden psychosis... a wire come loose? All she knew was his tone chilled her. To the very bone. Then he took out the knife. She recognised the kind. An Opinel camping knife, new by the looks, with the distinctive wooden handle and blade of hard carbon steel.

'Mack!' she said and fumbled for comms back to ElonGate.

'Don't bother. Everything's switched to the controls here. No-one will hear a word.'

She stared at him, unable to speak, near dead with fear.

'Now get it off. Everything. I've never seen a chink chick in the flesh before. And I'm way, way overdue.'

She knew her helmet was on the floor near her feet. She nudged it gently with her foot to make sure of where it was but did not take her eyes from his. She knew how to deal with dangerous dogs.

'Mack...' she tried again, if playing for time.

'Don't shit me. Just get it off.'

With one hand she snap-released the emergency override of her door. With the other she grabbed her helmet and gasping in a deep breath she tumbled from the rover, landing hard in the dust and rolling over and over, away down a little incline. Then she was on her feet running as fast as she could away. She didn't exhale... and kept running until she was over a little rise and got her helmet on before she could black out.

'What the fuck!!' Mack was screaming on their link. She muted him and ran. He could track her, but she could manoeuvre like the rover couldn't. She knew how to turn off her location transponder from a little hack a friend once showed her and did. Her location was now invisible to him. But her transponder was routed via the rover now – he had properly attended to that of course – so she was invisible to ElonGate too, and with comms switched to the rover she couldn't communicate with them, not even a distress call. She had an hour of oxygen, and calculated it was perhaps fifteen or so kilometres back to ElonGate. Even that distance, moving more slowly on Mars – it was simply harder to walk – might not be, she realised, possible... yet what choice did she have? She doubled back around through channels and gorges, watching for the rover. Although he could be on foot too now of course. In some ways it was an even more frightening prospect, being hunted by a lunatic across the face of Mars. She located the tracks they had left and started back, bearing in mind the faster she tried to go, the more oxygen she'd use up. She also knew he'd be well aware that following the tracks was the logical way for her to try to find her way back and come after her, so she was ever looking over her shoulder.

Her husband and children were back on Earth, and she reassured them in her daily family message that all was fine and good and she'd be home soon enough. It was a promise she never wanted to break to the man she'd loved nearly half her life… thoughtful, caring, undemanding Jerzy… and Finn, just nine, and Caitlin, only four. Four years old, and here her mother was, sacrificing two precious years of Caitlin's early childhood… that deepening sense of knowing the world, and of gaining a fuller knowledge of language… those first moments children start to realise the marks on a page correspond to written words, and thence to spoken language… and their joy in exploring nature with all its bugs and beetles, and the wonderment of seeing their first firefly. All of it sacrificed, for what? Tremors on Mars? Was she nuts? She had to be even crazier than McCluskey to have come to Mars at all. For what, she asked herself again? Scientific prestige? What was real and true and important in this life? She knew the answer could only be love. Of your family. Of another person who would sleep by you all your days and mingle their soul with yours in dreams. The love of your children, who came from your own body, watching them grow from a tiny helpless being into a tree climber then a teen rebel, then the young adult who strides the world with a confidence you can barely remember ever possessing yourself.

Half her oxygen supply was gone. Twenty-four minutes to get back. Twenty-four minutes of life left at the most, probably. She had no idea really how far it was to ElonGate but didn't dare switch her location finder back on, as then he could "see" her and find her. What had brought it on? He'd seemed "normal" enough before. Well, normal for him. She thought back to beery nights in the Mess and realised now how once or twice he'd momentarily left his unguarded eye on her. Now she knew that gaze for what it was. On their previous missions he'd been almost silent or oddly agitated, sometimes both at once. Yet he had seemed "OK", and professionally they had worked well as a team. He had always been careful, thorough, impeccably so. And they had always returned safely and "without issues". But now, what had happened? What had been the tripwire? Could it have been the talk of "Dark Matter", which seemed to infuriate him, unduly, irrationally so. There was the race thing too. He'd never shown any sign of that before, not the faintest. Now he had called her a "chink". It made her wonder if racism could hide out undetected in the brain stem, unknown perhaps even to the self, and lie dormant like a sleeper cell until it somehow got switched on. Did that turn the brain from grey matter to dark matter? The analogy and image were too neat, and despite her growing panic at her peril, she dismissed it with a grimace in her visor.

Nine minutes and still no sign of ElonGate. But it was ElonGate or death. In nine minutes. Only her training kept her breathing and moving, not just giving up in despair and sitting down to wait for death. If she did not get there, not only would she die, horribly, but all her memories of her family, the ones she loved, those memories would no longer exist either. And Jerzy and the children would be emotionally scarred for life. All because of one man's madness. Mars did bring out the worst in many of them. The unknown terrain of an alien world, and the equally alien terrain of their own minds. Psychologists were paid to listen to you talking about yourself, and psychiatrists were paid to listen to you talking about yourself and give you drugs. But in the end the demons were your own and you had to face them yourself. And McCluskey had lost that battle today, with his demons, for any of a myriad of reasons. Who knew the breaking point of a human, in the end, what it could do to them and what they could do to others? Because everyone had their inbuilt weaknesses, just as everyone had a different breaking point. And today he had broken, from a man she had thought a bit odd but basically decent into a knife-wielding lunatic rapist. Rape. Violation. The lowest act. Was there no end to human cruelty and perversity? It was Dark

62

Matter. It was true: it did make up so much of the world, the universe, and the human mind as well. The hidden part.

Night was falling now. And then, joyously, over the top of a rise she glimpsed the dull orange glow of ElonGate. Just one more hill parted her from it, and life. Could she do it in four minutes? Three and a half now? Panic rose in her throat. She was shaking hard. Three minutes and twenty seconds. Nineteen. She ran down and then up the last rise, and from it waved the one thing she could still use to communicate: a flashlight. She waved it high in the sky. The beam was powerful. Someone might see it. Must see it. She was so afraid her limbs barely moved on command. She knew she must go on. Even if they didn't see her waving light, she might just get there still…

She ran hard. Burning the last of her precious oxygen. Down to two minutes. One-fifty-eight. She heard her parents telling her to be brave. She heard her children's desperate cries, and Jerzy's soft-wept lament if she did not get there. She had to make it.

She became aware of something distant in the air, coming her way. Oh god let it be a drone. In that same moment the rover crossed her path, and stopped, blocking it.

'Hop in,' McCluskey said cheerily through a loudspeaker. 'Come on, it was just a survival exercise, OK? That went a bit too far. But funny too, don't you think?'

She stared at him.

'You've got less than a minute,' he said, as in the same instant she saw the rescue drone out of the corner of her eye. Would it get to her in time? She saw distant figures running in her direction.

'Nineteen seconds,' McCluskey said. 'Don't be stupid. Get in!'

She stood her ground, knowing she was looking at something that so many had sought for so long on this dead planet, and never found. She was looking into the eyes of an alien.

Location

'A lot of jobs in mining,' Roberto was saying. 'They pay plenty of money. The kind we can't imagine here. Literally out of this world.'

Ana's face remained immobile. 'You're a schoolteacher. And a good one. And... mining?'

'You do know, don't you, that you don't get down in there and do it yourself. You just supervise the robots doing it.'

'Yes I do know that. You don't even get a clipboard these days.'

He had to smile at that.

'But you know you really love teaching.' She topped up their glasses.

'I do. But how much longer will they need human teachers? Here or up there? And how long will we need lawyers, too? I can make us great money mining there. For the kids.'

'We'll need lawyers for about as long as people swindle each other, hit each other, kill each other and divorce,' she said. 'Some things we do tech can do, but what I do it can't.'

They'd had the argument more times than either of them could remember.

'There are courts up there too, you know.'

'One,' she said.

'So far. But the more people who go...'

The sound of a video commercial from the next room filled in the moment. It was for a chocolate bar. Some things never changed. The children were usually not very noisy, but tonight they were silent. They were listening, straining to hear over the manic music and voice-over of the advertisement, and both of them knew it.

'We could get good money for this place right now,' he said. 'The fresh breezes here up above the mud and heat, the view of the city and the bay, the...'

She sighed. 'Don't say it. Location. Yes, I know the value of our home too. But remember, that is what it is. Our home. Like this is our Earth. And these four walls are our very own place on the Earth. We have a house. And a good one. Yes, it's worth money…'

'Great money. If we sell right now.'

She shook her head and started carrying things to the sink. He got up and did the same.

The red lipstick of Ms Alvarez was impeccably applied, and her heels clicked across the cool parquetry as she displayed the Latest Releases to them on the big wall screen.

'You have a very nice office,' Roberto mentioned.

'Thank you.'

'And just off the Plaza de la Revolución, too,' Ana said.

'Yes we're pleased with our situation,' Ms Alvarez said.

'And the cross street is named after the man who led it… the founder of our country, in…when was it now…?' Ana remarked.

Ms Alvarez looked down toward her notes, and said nothing.

'… Yes, in 1821, ancient history now of course,' Roberto said, giving Ms Alvarez a reassuring smile.

She swivelled toward the screen and indicated locales of interest. 'Now, Elon Haven is the most attractive "satellite" settlement,' she said with a tiny smile, then added with an almost imperceptible downturn at the ends of her lips, 'and Elon Ville is also a very nice development, for those on a more… modest budget.' She was skilled enough not to look toward them as she said that. Roberto shifted slightly. Ana sat immobile.

'The Haven development as you may be aware is down in a major lava tube… and so it has optimum protection against…'

'Radiation,' Ana said.

'Yes. Although Ville has state of the art shielding too,' Ms Alvaez hastened to add.

'But not as good as being underground, is it,' Ana stated.

'One thing that is completely standard in both developments is radiation shielding of the highest standard, so please have no concerns whatever on those grounds, Mrs Fonseca. Haven or Ville, you and your children be as safe as in the executive Green Zone of ElonGate.'

'How big are they?' Roberto interceded.

'The standard domus in Haven is forty-five square metres. Ville is a little more constrained... thirty... but adequate, if cosy.'

'There are five of us,' Ana said.

'Congratulations on what I'm sure is a very lovely family. Schools are incorporated into each development of course. Creches, clinics, gyms. All there.'

'But that standard is better in Haven, I take it,' Ana said.

'A little, yes. But of course there are lovely views up in Ville.' She showed a video pan of orange-red plains spreading out into the basin of a lofty range. 'Spectacular, no?'

'So on Mars the better off live down below, and the rest are up above. A kind of reverse of the rich living up on the hill,' Ana said. 'But I know, in this world and even on that one, you only ever get what you pay for.'

Ms Alvarez knew the situation. If there was one thing those in her line of work knew, it was people, families and their complexities. It was her job to navigate the swell and chop of those to the safe harbour of the sale.

'And tell me,' Ana went on, 'just say I wanted to pop back for a shopping trip. How far is Mars from Earth and how long would it take me to get back here from there?'

'Oh well, now that you're asking,' Ms Alvarez smiled, 'I'm not sure. I mean I should know how far it is and how long it takes... I could look it up.' She laughed then, showing small glittering teeth that looked newly budded in their bright pink gums. 'A girl can't live without her Prada, can she? And they don't have proper stores up there yet. That I do know for a fact. But they will, soon, soon.'

'It's around six to nine months travel time dear, as I suspect you may have heard somewhere along the line,' Roberto said quietly. 'They work it so you fly when the planets are closest together. They orbit at different

66

speeds... it's all pretty complex. But that's what we have scientists and computers for, rocket science.'

Ms Alvarez smiled yet again at that. She displayed a limited but reliable range. Gracious. Warmly professional. Genuinely amused. Slightly condescending, but not so much so that clients would ever pick it. And, like every person in her trade, the social lubricant smile. The one she wore now.

'Pricing?' Roberto asked.

'The standard domus in Haven comes in at 200,000 US dollars. In Ville it's 130. Neither is inclusive of add-ons of course, like carpets and appliances and so on. Our floor coverings range from rush matting up to fine Oriental rugs, appliances up to designer chic, all depending on your budget and taste, as well as light fittings, paint finish and so-on. There are other special extras if you wish too, such as an extension conservatory where you can grow your own plants. They're very popular... and the price of decontam soil is falling now too. Of course, we predict significant capital growth as you would effectively be getting in on the ground floor, so to speak. With more and more settlers arriving all the time the graph goes up and up into the wide blue sky. And whoever thought you'd find that on Mars.'

They all smiled at the obviously well-oiled remark. 'Anyway, if you are interested,' and here she glanced in Ana's direction, 'I'll send you all the details, so you can both go through it at your leisure at home. And please feel free to get back to me if you'd like more information, another meeting... whatever you wish.'

Roberto looked across at Ana. Her face clearly said little.

'Yes please, Ms Alvarez,' he said, 'please send it all to us.'

She gave them her warm professional smile. 'Please, call me Felicia.'

'And are you?' Roberto asked.

'What?'

'Lucky. That's what your name means.'

'Oh, well,' she laughed, 'you know I couldn't say that. It might bring me bad luck.'

That night Roberto scraped the dinner plates and stacked the dishwasher. About an hour later they put the children to bed and went back downstairs to the kitchen and opened a second bottle of wine.

'Well,' Ana said at length, 'I say we go.'

'Really?' He didn't even try to disguise his surprise.

'Everyone says Mars is the future. And I'm sure there'll be work for me there, even if not in the law to start with. And if you're getting paid the kinds of money you've mentioned, the children's futures will be assured, so it's the responsible thing to do. Whereas staying here…'

She sipped and looked at him.

'Haven or Ville?' he asked.

'I think we could just maybe do Haven, don't you? But I don't think with what we'd get for this place, even in the current market, we'd be able to afford the top of the range add-ons.'

'Pity,' he said, at length. 'I've always lusted after a German dishwasher.'

Ana smiled. 'Almost as much as Ms Alvarez lusts for her Prada.'

Roberto kissed her. 'You're so smart, my darling. It's true. How could I leave here, when so many clearly still know so little? And you're dealing with so many swindlers.'

'True. And yes, I'm kind of attached to what I do. Like you.'

She poured two more glasses, and they raised them in a toast, clinked and drank.

The Book of Samuel

'The foie gras is really rather good tonight,' Mrs Catherine Parker is saying to everyone and no-one in particular, dangling her flute for the waiter to top up with bubbly. 'Which is just as well after last night's catastrophe of one.' The bejewelled and imperious Mrs Parker, as she insists on being called, rules this little realm as our own Catherine the Great. To my eyes she'd be the first accused in an Agatha Christie murder mystery, which is often how this cruise feels to me. I'm perched down the Siberian end of the long table because I'm a callow youth of 27, no-one in particular and certainly not rich, but it's my job to be here. There are other young people on board, but nearly all of them are crew: cooks, stewards, cleaners, maintenance workers, engineers. It's all very select: a little more than two hundred souls on board, about half of them passengers, the rest catering to their whims.

'For what we're paying, the foie gras damn well oughta be "really rather good" too!' Beau "Bobo" Nelson declares with his grin across the candle-lit expanse, imploring puppy-eyed for us all to join in. Every cruise has a Bobo. Ours is no mere clown though: he's a shrewd leisurewear billionaire from Tampa played by Slim Pickens, with his Sissy Spacek bride nodding in his shadow. A few at the table agree with him, up to a fair and reasonable point, but Mrs Parker herself does not deign. Mostly Mrs Parker doesn't deign, especially to me. For one thing there's my dinner suit. She never deigns to that, not a glance. She merely gives me her sees-nothing-sees-all yogic eye and calls me "young Sammy".

Mrs Parker is an impeccably curated 60-year-old from Sydney, a woman of seemingly non-surgical residual youth, with status needs she sates with the relentlessness of a hamster in a mill. Her husband is here too, just, the mouse in her pocket. Mrs Parker looks away to the Captain's table, where our commander sits in his fine dress uniform, gleaming with its real brass buttons, at the head of his officers and the most select passengers. She watches the captain at his table with a kind of yearning, and everything in her husband's face says they will never make it, and it will all be his fault.

On one rare occasion she did deign to speak to me, Mrs Parker asked with apparent warmth and interest, 'And what is it you actually *do*, young Sammy?' I explained I write branded content for tour companies, hotels and resorts and the like on travel sites. 'And what is "branded content", please?' she asked, and I endeavoured to explain the permeable line between marketing and journalism. I mentioned this was obviously my biggest assignment by far, and she patted my hand and moved on. I couldn't help but think if she found me more interesting and attractive, my position at the table might change.

'Well we've got no complaints so far, do we dear?' old Mr dos Santos says. He's a retired judge from Colombo, and he and his wife have spent their life savings on this cruise. He has hairs so long and thick sprouting from his ears that you could plait them, and I wonder why so many old people seem happy to inflict their decrepitude on others. Even with all the things doctors can do now people still get old, and like nearly every other passenger on the ship, they're old. Who else do you meet on cruises, especially one like this, but rich old farts?

I rhapsodise about the ship and its amenities in my content posts. The *Reeve* after all is the pride of the line: sleek and sharp and gleaming white outside and in. She's the biggest and fanciest such liner in service. Everything you could wish for on a luxury cruise is laid on with a trowel: cabins designer-fussed, the finest foods and wines, and the line's famous personal service. There's a nightly live show, too, a trio of performers doing everything from stand-up and drag to snippets of Shakespeare and Wilde. The female of the group is a beguiling Nigerian called Aria, and somehow I have become her lover.

Aria is a year or two younger than me and renowned as an exotic dancer in Paris and Berlin, a kind of contemporary Josephine Baker. At least one in this line of showbiz is considered *de rigueur* for cruises.

She's Ophelia one night, a magician's assistant the next, the magician the night after, a stripper, a juggler, and a comedian. No-one could say Aria isn't versatile, as I have learnt myself. Our eyes met over the bain-marie while I was looking at the crew facilities, and the rest is graphic content.

Part of my brief is to emphasise the "uber cool fun" to be had on this cruise. Keeping the pampered passengers happy, entertained and satiated all the time is no mean feat for the crew on a trip as long as this one. Every movie ever made, every song recorded, every online game will only get you so far. There are retro amusements like deck quoits and darts, macrame and crocheting for the wild at heart, and of course, there's the colossus himself, Atlas, the Pilates instructor. He does his darndest to keep his large, almost exclusively female clientele stretched and satisfied. There are information sessions too of course, about what awaits us when we arrive. Interest in those has waned, but will inevitably pick up as we approach our destination.

One thing I enjoy is our daily stroll along the Deck, past passengers sprawled on deck chairs beneath their finely tuned low-UV sun lamps, gazing into the starry deeps. This is a special design feature of the *Reeve*: its enormous observation windows where the wellness advisors hope the passengers may find themselves in calming contemplation of the empyrean.

I am jolted from my thoughts by Mrs Parker addressing me directly. 'Well young Sam, it would appear the show is about to start. I wonder who the focal point will be tonight? I do hope it's your young lady. She is rather pretty and quite talented, but if you ask me those two chaps only ever really enjoy lip-synching to Shirley Bassey.'

This strikes me as an unfair, even bigoted statement, as Jerry and Benny are perfectly adequate and professional in everything they do. The trio have been selected for endurance as much as anything else – including enduring passengers like Mrs Parker. I smile back at her as minimally best as I can, and desserts arrive. The room lights go down and the little stage at the end of the room lights up with Aria in a surgical gown being pushed out on a hospital bed, groaning comically and making grotesque faces and screaming out, 'Oh… oh… god!!'. Then from beneath her gown she "gives birth" to a soft toy rabbit, held up high by a white-coated doctor. 'Ello, ello, ello!' declares the doctor, 'so who got a very special visit from the Easter Bunny this year, eh?'

Bobo laughs broadly, Mrs Parker harrumphs and Mr and Mrs dos Santos look down. 'Caint please everyone I guess,' Bobo winks at me. 'Besides your gal's doin' helluva lot better than just some dumb bunny, ain't she Sam!' he declares, and Sissy nudges him. I wonder what the show director will get Aria to flash from under her hem next. 'But hey, that's entertainment, ain't it Sam,' Bobo laughs, and the dos Santoses peer into the lees of their claret like tea leaf readers seeking tomorrow but finding only dregs.

When I wake, Aria's form – I have to stop myself thinking "heavenly body" – lies unveiled by the sheet like a flesh and blood Rodin, her lips smiling at my blinking eyes.

'Good morning sleepy head.'

'Already?'

'Past ten. Or whatever.'

The night before returns. Shots at the bar, the two of us the last to leave as the waiters indeed whistle as it closes. Again. Somehow the booze never lays a paw on Aria, who always looks like a teetotaller who's slept ten hours. Me on the other hand, I know I look like a sack of offal on a barge on the Thames.

Somehow that doesn't dim Aria's smile. 'I had a great time last night.'

'I wish I could remember it. You're always so wonderful.'

'No, you are.'

'No, you are,' I tease, and we laugh. I am as ever enthralled by her. She is lean and strong and she is cool, calm and very fine, her every movement a dance. I wonder what she sees in a lumpy white lad from Clapham, but it must be something because here she is beside me, looking into my eyes as if there's something of worth in them.

'How do you handle those old bores every night?' she asked me.

'I console myself it won't go on forever. Is that how you feel about those two guys?'

She locates a half-drunk glass of scotch by the bed, takes a sip and passes it to me. 'They got the gig because one of them was fucking the director.'

'I knew there must be something in the woodheap.'

'They're very nice boys, really.'

'Just not very good.'

'Eyes and teeth, eyes and teeth,' she grins, 'half of showbiz.'

We are by now fondling significant parts of the other.

'By the way,' she murmurs, 'have you heard there are three people in the infirmary?'

'The foie gras or the caviar?'

'Mmm,' she says.

The next day I get a summons to the bridge. I find Captain Mishra a bit of an odd fellow. NASA-trained and highly proficient, yes, but it's as if he's always thinking of something else when he speaks to me. Perhaps he's like that with everyone, I don't know. Now his face shows the kind of concern a commander is meant to conceal beneath a gloss of right stuff.

'You've heard rumours of an outbreak?' he says after brief pleasantries.

'Only that there are some people in the infirmary.'

'Two dead already,' he states. 'And five more down with it.'

'Jesus…. I just thought it must be the food or something.'

'No.'

'So what is it?'

'We don't know yet, though we believe it's viral. It seems to start with a fever and seizures, then a terrible delirium sets in. It becomes ever more extreme, and death comes from heart failure. It can all be over in hours. The doctors can't work out why it's appearing now, so many months into the voyage. Their guess is an asymptomatic case embarked with us from Earth, and it's been circulating, incubating and slowly degrading our immune systems all this time. And now it's coming for us. Mortality is a hundred percent so far. All elderly passengers though. One crew member is down too and the doctors are hopeful she may survive because of her youth, but who knows? If she does and still has her sanity intact after the delirium, that's another thing.'

'This… delirium. What happens?'

'No patient has come out of it enough yet to tell. We've sealed off the infirmary now, but people may already have heard something.'

'Heard what?'

'Demonic howls. Bellows. Screams. We can't know what they're seeing in their hallucinations, but whatever it is…'

'Will we get to ElonGate?' I hear myself ask.

'Oh, we'll get there all right. This ship can fly itself all the way and even land of its own accord. But whether any of us will be alive by then is another matter.'

I take it all in as best I can. 'Why are you telling me?'

He hands me something. It's a long time since I've held a real printed book, and this one is old, very, with romantically yellowing pages that rustle like autumn leaves. It is *A Journal of the Plague Year* by Daniel Defoe.

'Do you know it?' he asks.

'Yes. I've read it. A long time ago now.'

'I suggest you read it again. And keep a journal of your own.'

'OK, but just so you know, I'm no Dafoe.'

'Well now you could be.'

'You do know it's a work of fiction, don't you Captain?'

'Yes. But the Plague wasn't.'

'And you… just happened to bring it along on this trip?'

'No. It's in the ship's library, I think for just in case. This is the just in case.' He hands me a blank notebook and a pen. 'Ink on paper is best,' he says.

I start my journal that day. On the next the dos Santoses die. Both go just a few hours after getting the first symptoms, mercifully as it turns out. The Captain officiates at a short, sombre service before their bodies are ejected into space, the grandest necropolis. Their vacant places at our table are hard to cover up with platitudes. Bobo remains relentlessly upbeat, but Mrs Parker's expression leads me to wonder if she suspects the outbreak is the result of some sort of cabal or conspiracy. Most of the faces at our table are blankly terrified, but they still need feeding and their proprietors eat without ceremony and go.

Two nights later the Captain makes a speech to the passengers and crew, so that there's not a person on board who doesn't know our circumstances first-hand. We become only too aware that we are in a tiny capsule hurtling through deep space, with many millions of kilometres still to go to Mars, and a lethal virus rampant on board. The Captain tells us one thing we already know anyway, that there's no way anyone on Earth, the moon or Mars can reach and help us. We are on our own.

The cruise company has an officially approved plan for such an outbreak, but over the following weeks we find that none of the normal countermeasures, of quarantine, isolation and the rest, make the slightest difference. Passengers keep falling sick and dying. A few of the younger crew members do survive the illness, but remain bedridden afterwards, severely confused and disoriented. They need constant care with feeding, changing soiled bed clothes, and most of all someone to comfort them with physical contact and gentle words. The eyes of these rare survivors are hollow, as if their souls have been wrenched out through the pupils. It's all they can do to have the most basic verbal exchange. For those in the throes of the illness, dispensing analgesics for the fever remains our only treatment. It feels criminally inadequate.

Soon more staff, younger and stronger, start to fall ill too. The three doctors and all the nursing staff die, unable to avoid infection no matter what precautions they took, leading us to wonder again if infection goes back to our departure from Earth. Then the first officer goes mad and murders Captain Mishra bellowing that he's part of an alien plot, and flees in an escape pod, shrieking alone into the maw of space. The ship feels rudderless after that, even as it flies on toward Mars.

We survivors eat in our rooms whatever we can scavenge from the kitchens. No cleaning is done. Filthy laundry moulders in hallways, the pervading smell is like stale cabbage and cat urine. We have to stop bathing to save water when the recycling plant breaks down and no-one can fix it properly, not even Bobo who's always ready to try his hand at anything. The infirmary is abandoned and the sick die in their rooms, their last howls and cries barely muffled behind their doors, and after that all we can do is seal them in to try to keep the sickening stink of rotting flesh away. Almost inevitably, some people go on a binge and down the entire stock of champagne, the corridors run with wine and vomit no-one cleans up. Luckily there's a large locked store of spirits which we hope will last us.

Amid all the chaos the one thing that does go on is the nightly show. Even after Aria's two fellow performers fall ill, we emerge from our rooms and she dances for us. We all start to look forward to her ever more outrageous routines, women and men alike… even me, and I'm sleeping with her. But other than for her performances we rarely leave my room, spending our time talking and reading and making love, with as little time as possible "out" foraging. One day Aria tells me she's pregnant, and the one after that she feels unwell. I hope it's routine, to do with the pregnancy, but it isn't. In a few hours her temperature soars to 40 degrees and she writhes as if possessed, howling with eyes like nuggets of fire, and racked with seizures that leave the bed linen sopping with her sweat. But at least she is fighting it, for the lives of both of them.

Days pass. I record more in my journal about the young who survive, desperate for any indication Aria might too. After the infection passes, their condition seems improved if they receive reassurance during the most vivid and terrible of the hallucinations, almost as if one becomes their guide on a bad acid trip. I become that for Aria, and in the blessed interludes from the delirium, she asks me to read her to her. Usually she wants Shakespeare's Sonnets. Once though she asks for something from *A Journal of the Plague Year*. As I leaf through its pages, I recall how Captain Mishra pressed it into my hand, seemingly so long ago.

'It pleased God that I was still spared,' I read as she lies twitching and glazed with sweat, but at least quiet for now, 'and very hearty and sound in health, but very impatient of being pent up within doors without air, as I had been for fourteen days or thereabouts; and I could not restrain myself, but I would go to carry a letter for my brother to the post-house. Then it was indeed that I observed a profound silence in the streets.'

'Silent streets,' Aria whispers, 'corridors, rooms.'

I nod and go on. 'When I came to the post-house, as I went to put in my letter I saw a man stand in the corner of the yard and talking to another at a window, and a third had opened a door belonging to the office. In the middle of the yard, lay a small leather purse with two keys hanging at it, with money in it, but nobody would meddle with it. I asked how long it had lain there; the man at the window said it had lain almost an hour, but that they had not meddled with it, because they did not know if the person who dropped it might come back to look for it, or to get the money at the hazard it might be attended with.'

'So... nearness of death... makes people honest,' she breathes.

'Something like that, I suppose.'

'I love you.' Somehow she smiles. 'Honestly.'

'I love you too and you're not going to die. You're both going to live. We three are.'

She smiles again and closes her eyes, and another seizure hits her.

Not long after this I record something truly disturbing. The empty-eyed young who survive seem to last only another a few weeks more, and then slip into a coma and die. I can't work it out. The illness is gone. It isn't that. In the end I come to the conclusion that whatever torture they have endured has extracted the most precious filament from them: the will to live.

It feels extremely dangerous to venture out at all now, as the corridors are filled with stinking, rotting corpses, and people in the worst, late throes of the illness, and I have already witnessed survivors being attacked by the sick, believing them part of their hallucinations. The cries and moans, the shrieks and screams, are ceaseless now, maddening in their own way to the rest of us, and the walkways of the once lavish *Reeve* are mired in rubbish, filth and excrement, and ever more bodies that have been left to rot where they have fallen because there is no-one to dispose of them. The overwhelming stink of human decay is all around us, and the few who remain well can do nothing but stay in their rooms and try to avoid it, and the illness itself.

But I must forage, though food supplies are dwindling. In the corridor, of all people I come across Mrs Parker, carrying supplies and scurrying along.

'Sam…' she says, and breaks into tears that only weeks ago would have been unthinkable for her. 'Sam, you're alive!'

'So are you,' I grin, struck by who the illness takes, and who it seems to leave. I've been racking my brains for any thread, but there doesn't seem to be one.

'Bobo is well too.'

'Really?'

'Yes… he's… well you see, our spouses are gone… so we circled the wagons, so to speak. We're together in my cabin.'

The idea of Mrs Parker and Bobo together anywhere seems almost too bizarre, but then we are trapped in a blink of light in deep space with nearly everyone else dead or mad.

'Do you happen to know if anyone is still in charge of this thing?' I ask her.

'Bobo says one engineer is still up on the bridge. A very reliable young woman too, he says. You do know we reach Mars in two days don't you.'

'No,' I murmur, not quite able to take it in. 'No, I… didn't know that.'

'They know everything about us on Mars of course,' she says. 'Bobo says he just hopes they help guide us down and don't let us crash and burn or just leave us to die where we land in the ship. To protect themselves.'

I hadn't thought of that. 'Surely not.'

'There are fifteen thousand colonists in ElonGate now,' she says. 'Think of it, if this virus got in there.'

'But surely they'll just quarantine us.'

'For how long? No-one even knows what this is yet.'

Of all things then, we hear music. It seems to be coming from the dining room. I recognise the song: Nina Simone, *Sinnerman*, and I know who loves that song. Mrs Parker follows a few paces behind me as we navigate past the dead and dying and enter the room where we see the astonishing spectacle of Aria dancing naked on the tiny stage.

'Aria!' I call out, but she seems not to hear. In the same moment I see two other people in the room... Bobo, who grins a greeting, and a little way off from him a young woman I presume to be the surviving engineer Mrs Parker mentioned. How many others are left alive on board I can't guess, but it's probably fewer than twenty, maybe even ten, and from the sounds we've heard many of those may be sick too. We could even be the last healthy people on the ship.

I see Mrs Parker's hand touch Bobo's. The young woman glances up at me with a look that says don't come any closer. Meanwhile the song goes into the instrumental break, with its primal, tapping, racing heartbeat, and Aria is leaping, whirling and soaring above us. Although I'm deeply worried about the reserves she must be calling on to dance, I can't help but love the grace and majesty of this woman who of all things seems to be mine, as I am hers, and we three are us. Aria appears to have no grasp of where she is, and deep in the grip of delirium dances ever faster, her face alive with something like transcendence as it spins and she yells out *'Power!!'* again and again and again, amid a blur of arms flying around her head.

She seems to be telling a story, of all the peoples of the Earth, dancing their legends and tales, each in its own spinning orb. The vision is gripping and potent, and we seem to be in kind of group trance, and see on her face and body the faces and hair and paint and dress of the peoples of

Asia, of Africa, Europe, of the Americas, the Pacific, of Australia… and then the visions seem to change… and as she dances ever more frenetically we see raging seas, erupting volcanoes, caves and ancient rock paintings, and I seem to see long strands of written words issuing from her open mouth, from the 23rd Psalm, Dante's *Inferno*, *Faust*… and I wonder if we aren't infected too… and then I see… perhaps all four of us see… what seem like random images spinning from her hands… a baby, an atom, a cat, a flower, a skeleton, a cow, a tree, a jackal…

In a flash I know what she is doing, and rush forward to try to stop her, but she shoves me back as she spins so that I fall back onto a table and chairs and she keeps dancing as the song nears its climax. Now I am truly frightened and know I must put an end to this death dance. I call to the others, 'Help me, please!' but they seem frozen, spellbound, and this time Aria gets me with a wild, high kick and I go down again, hard. The song climaxes with its final blaring, glaring chords, racing beat and bashing of cymbals, and what appears to be a plume of yellow-green bile that turns into blood, which sprays from her mouth as the last crystal piano notes cascade down a falls and subside into a pool of silence. Aria appears to wilt then, she totters from that tawdry little stage and collapses onto the floor beside me, and fastening my arm in her searing grip, dies.

I must have passed out, and wake to find myself being cared for by Mrs Parker and Bobo in their room. Or at least, that's who I recognise them as, at first. As time goes on and my infection takes a deeper hold, like tentacles stretching through my innards and toying with my brain, I have no idea who they are except their faces transmute from Buddhas into gurus into demons, into the lions and monkeys I had in my box of playthings as a boy. A cup is placed to my lips and a voice says 'Drink, Sam,' and I think, who is Sam and why the hell wouldn't he want to drink? Is he on the wagon? A teetotaller? What the fuck then is the matter with Sam? But I comply and drink, even if it's only stupid water with some pill in it, and I wonder who even bothers drinking fucking water? What is the drinking purpose of water? As I picture the word "purpose" I see a porpoise somehow holding a tumbler of scotch in its hand.

I am nowhere. Naked in space. All is black, but right below my bared feet is the Red Planet, Mars. Right there. But there is no way I can get down to it. I am floating in space, dangling, unable to move. And all around me unseen eyes are watching, every little thing I do. I can't see them, but I know they're there all right. I feel the way I did when I crossed the checked carpeted floor of the bar in that Howard Johnson's that Thursday night in Houston, and there was a crooner in a bow tie by the piano who made me want to puke and everyone at the bar was chatting each other up with dagger eyes and foot-long tongues down each other's throats scooping out the insides like runny ice cream, and I saw it all and wanted to run but knew I had to just keep walking across that checked carpet, spongy as the suspension of an old Dodge, because I knew I was here for a purpose, only now I can't remember what it was. I stopped walking and stood there in the middle of that carpet in the middle of that room in the middle of all that nothing, and yelled. 'What is my porpoise here?? *What??* What is my porpoise?? Fucking… *water??*' And somehow, from somewhere, a voice answers, 'Yes, Sam. Now drink it.'

I return somewhat to my senses on final descent. Below I see a low-slung scape of what looks like the dusted burbs of Los Angeles from the air, scratched from desert. These I dimly think to be the neat rows of Elon-Gate, the colony that the *Reeve* has travelled so many millions of kilometres to reach. The ship functions smoothly and sets itself down with a feather touch. The engines shut down and are silent. I sit there a moment and realise that somehow I have arrived. I look around and see there are three other people on the bridge, Mrs Parker, Bobo and the young engineer. Sadly, the couple look dead and the engineer asleep. I realise then she looks familiar and remember. We had a drink one night soon after departure from Earth, and I liked her. Polly, was it? But then I met Aria.

Figures in full hazmat suits are here now.

'The young woman…?' I manage to ask.

'No,' a voice from the suit says. 'You're the only one left.'

I try to remember her name. Dolly? Or was it Molly?

'But she got you safely down,' the voice says.

'I thought the ship did that by itself...'

'Not in the state this one's in,' the voice says. 'She landed it. And saved you.'

'Thank you Polly... Molly... no, no... it was Holly. Holly.' Then I think a moment, looking around. 'And Bobo, and Mrs Parker. Thank you both too.'

As they lift me up they tell me I had something in my hand when they reached me, and hand it back to me.

'It's my journal, of our journey,' I tell them.

They take me down a chute onto the surface. Red dirt I see, then sleep and dream for what feels like forever.

Everyone on Mars

He was a dirty man. Very dirty. Everyone said so even though no-one really knew who everyone was. But the universal view was he was a Very Dirty Man. A new arrival might ask is he dirty because of a lack of personal hygiene, habits, or his behaviour toward others? No one knew exactly, but the common wisdom abided that he was dirty. Very.

Why so many people took an interest in a man no-one really seemed to know was a mystery. It meant they were constantly being scandalised by the repute of one not in their own circle, nor even in their daily lives. But still they whispered in the corridors and roared over drinks and chatted tirelessly online about the Very Dirty Man. People gasped at stories others told. It did not seem possible such a person could exist in their midst in this day and age.

When he shopped, someone would inevitably mutter 'there goes the dirty man', and a companion would respond 'Yes, yes, he's dirty all right. Very.' But children overhearing could be confused. He didn't look dirty to them – his clothing, skin and hair appeared clean, so why did adults call him dirty? One day a girl asked her mother directly: 'Why do you say he is dirty, when he doesn't look at all dirty?' To which the mother replied: 'His dirt is not the kind you can see.' Which left the child more confused than ever.

At the weekly dance a woman turned her heel and fell. The place was crowded and rowdy, with plenty of drink, and only one or two others half-noticed, but the person who went to her aid was the Very Dirty Man. He extended his hand to help her up, but to his surprise she refused to take it.

'What is the matter?'

'I won't take your hand, sir.'

'Why not? Is there a problem?'

'Yes, there is.'

'What is it then, madam?'

She hesitated before going on. 'I could never touch a dirty man, especially a very dirty one.' But the words sounded odd out loud, even as she spoke them.

He appeared surprised. 'Who says I am dirty?'

'Oh,' she said, 'everyone.'

He considered this. 'And, who is everyone?'

'Well, everyone is everyone,' she went on, although her voice was sounding odd now to her own ears, alien even.

'So if I ask anyone, would they say the same thing about me? That I'm a dirty man?'

'I suppose so,' she answered, if a little less readily now.

'But if everyone thinks that, then if I ask anyone, isn't that the same thing?' he reasoned. 'Because in that view of things, anyone is really just a little cog of everyone. And that means you as anyone, are also everyone.'

'I had never quite thought of it quite like that. But yes, perhaps that's true.'

'So do you think I am a dirty man? Very dirty?'

She regarded him but did not speak, and now took his proffered hand to help her up. As she dusted herself off she noticed a dark mark where her hem had fallen onto her spilled glass of red wine.

'Oh,' she said. 'Look, I've stained my dress.'

He fetched a glass of water and handed it to her to try to wash the mark out.

'That's funny really,' she said at length, slowing her rubbing, seemingly making little further attempt to wash the mark away.

'Why do you say that?'

'Because now I'm dirty too. And curiously enough I can't think of you as a dirty man any more. And certainly not very dirty.'

'Why not?'

She thought a moment. 'Well… I suppose it means I now suspect that everyone might be wrong. Which until this moment I had not believed possible.'

'Well I for one don't know what everyone thinks,' he replied. 'I can only know what you think and I think.'

After that they all had so much more to talk about. Not only did they have a very dirty man in their midst, now they had a dirty woman too. Whether she was very dirty remained moot. Any sighting of them together only heightened the fascination, and every tiny detail was dissected, analysed and debated. There was also much salacious speculation about the kinds of things that might go on between them behind closed doors. The lack of any information at all about that only intensified things. All anyone knew was he was a Very Dirty Man, and now she was probably well on the way to becoming a Very Dirty Woman. And whatever went on between them must by definition be dirty. Very.

Everyone knew that. Everyone on Mars.

Science Fiction

My name is Sonya Nyerere and I am a historian. Some may have heard of me, possibly even read one of my works, but most probably have not.

Part of the task of the historian is to render events as a formal chronicle for scholars, but I see it as an even greater duty to relate events in a manner most people can readily grasp.

So it is that I set down this brief account in the form of a short story. The few pieces of dialogue are from primary sources and are included for the fuller knowledge and understanding of the general reader.

Dee and Derek Jones were pioneers. They were among the first actual migrants to ElonGate, meaning they were not part of science, research or mining, nor were they intending to return and live back on Earth again. Mars was their new home. They were professional climbers, and their dream was to start the first climbing business on the mountainous planet. Inevitably the first few years were hard, but with traffic gradually increasing from Earth their fortunes were beginning to show signs of a turn for the better when tragedy struck. Attempting to rescue a reckless, stranded client, Derek died in a fall. Dee was left not only devastated and bereft, but alone in charge of a struggling business on the alien world they had chosen as their home. The company had some twenty employees at the time and she did not know if it would survive. But then the holiday and cruise market started up and, with rising demand, Martian Expeditions gradually began to show a return, and to prosper. Before too long it had fifty people on the payroll, then a hundred. Mars turned out to be as good for business as she and Derek had dreamed. The company established a strong reputation and ever more clients were prepared to pay the big fees to climb. They were, after all, billionaires.

Dee became the founding CEO of the ElonGate Chamber of Commerce, declaring she was proud the planet's first such body was headed by a woman. With her growing repute, she successfully petitioned the administration for the name of the one mountain the company was authorised to climb to be changed from Mount Cupertino to Mount Derek. By Martian standards, Mount Derek was a molehill. Compared to Olympus Mons, at more than 20,000 metres high, Derek barely cleared its ankle, at 2,000 metres. It was a good climb though, demanding just enough skill and athleticism to keep most customers satisfied.

But the day came that changed everything. Dee and her head climber, Tora Lindvig, were preparing to take a group of Indian and Japanese climbers up the summit. The group was more adventurous than many. All four had summited Everest, K2 and many other peaks back on Earth. They had studied the route, considered it lame, and wanted to take a new way up. Derek was a craggy peak, which made it more interesting to climb, but finding a new route was a challenge. Dee asked them if they were sure… it would mean a delay… and they left her in no doubt they did not want to follow any well-worn, touristed route up. They wanted a real climb and would pay a generous bonus for it. For the figure they offered she couldn't argue, but she said it would take at least a week while she ascended it with Tora, mapped out the new route, and repeated the ascent to check it. They agreed.

Tora was Norwegian, a born climber, up for anything. She was also ten years younger than Dee, which was both a boon and a liability. Climbing was difficult enough even in the latest suits, but Tora treated it like a stroll up a rise. Dee always remembered what Derek used to say: over-confidence is the enemy of any climber. He was always respectful of any peak and very careful, and even he had died. She worried for Tora, but the Norwegian always seemed to take any challenge, hitch, problem in her stride.

They left Base Pod soon after breakfast and arrived at the proposed route up the South Face. Tora had already climbed it alone, against company rules. Scanning it, Dee was impressed but wondered if it might not be just too challenging. Tora assured her it was exactly what the tech titan clients wanted for bragging rights back home.

The first section was relatively easy going, but then came a far steeper, near-vertical part and up above Dee, Tora started knocking in pitons. Soon they were climbing hard, fingers searching out crevices in the rock, and Dee was starting to think the route might be too difficult after all for non-professionals, when something very curious happened. Reaching into a crevice to pull herself past a jutting section of rock, her gloved hand touched something soft. It was the strangest sensation she'd had in six years climbing on Mars. She felt it again. It wasn't just accumulated dust, she realised. It was squishy.

'Come on Dee!' Tora called down. 'What's the hold-up?'

'I think... I need you to come down here,' Dee called back.

'Why? Are you OK?'

'Just do it please.'

She heard a grunt of assent and in a few moments Tora was down beside her.

'What is it?' She saw Dee's hand still in a crevice. 'Caught?'

'No. There's something... well... soft... and... squishy in here. It feels like it could be... some kind of slime.'

'You're kidding, right?'

'No.'

'Have you looked in there?'

'I can't see in.'

'Well come on, get your glove out! It could be... I dunno... eating your hand or something.'

Dee slowly withdrew it from the crevice. A sticky, slimy substance adhered to her glove, and their eyes widened to see it was a vivid, iridescent, dazzling blue, glistening in the light.

'Whoa,' Tora breathed. 'Science fiction.'

Teams rushed to Mount Derek and the confirmation was made. The news was flashed back to Earth. All the slime was meticulously collected and stored. Back in the lab in ElonGate, scientists monitored it, hoping it would survive what they assumed was the trauma of being moved. They watched breathlessly as very slowly, by the millimetre, it congealed. After several days it had assumed the form of a neat round blob like a bright blue cowpat, and roughly that size. At the same time an intensive search was conducted on Mount Derek and in the surrounding area, but no more slime was found. Scientists pondered the bizarre proposition that it was somehow unique. That defied logic. But despite the decades of human presence on Mars now, it was the only sign of life yet found.

The first tentative research was undertaken. Imaging revealed something surprising. Nothing. Somehow, it was impervious to scanning. That was so bizarre that at first few could accept it. Scientists were stumped. Some argued there was so much they could learn if they just took even the most minute sample and analysed it, but caution overruled that. Any physical interference could harm it. It must have some outer defensive layer, scientists reasoned – perhaps even a force field – that denied or confused image probing.

It was avidly monitored for months. Nothing seemed to happen. Everything about it was intriguing. What was it doing? Was it even alive? What was it living on? It eventually emerged it was taking in small amounts of carbon dioxide. Was it somehow "breathing" CO2 or, like plants, was it somehow photosynthesising with available artificial light? But they didn't even know yet if it had a cellular structure. On Earth, plants photosynthesised CO2 and water, using the energy from sunlight their leaves collected to produce energy and carbohydrates for their cells. The plant grew, flourished and eventually died. But how was this subsisting? Its home atmosphere was composed almost entirely of CO2, but in the crevice where they had found it there was a maximum of just three hours of weak sunlight falling on it a day… light about half the intensity of that on Earth. That part of the equation at least worked to a degree… CO2 and sunlight. But what about the water? There was a minute trace of water vapour in the atmosphere… but could that be enough, with all the CO2? And could the organism even absorb sunlight without any obvious leaves? It bamboozled them. They just looked at it and shook their heads, and it did nothing but sit in its glass case. Eventually there were questions about whether the resources on Mars were equal to the task, and the proposition put that the full battery of technology available on Earth was needed.

The debate in the scientific community was long, passionate and acrimonious. One side said it was crucial for the future of humanity to know what this thing was. The majority argued that as important to science as it might be, it was certainly not worth gambling the future of Earth by bringing it back. One side called the other alarmist and lacking in scientific courage and the other retorted that to bring it to Earth would be the height of recklessness.

Earth's online realm became fascinated by the "Cutest Critter", as it was dubbed, and the overwhelming majority wanted to see it brought from Mars. The media saw a good story and backed it in. The argument raged, with celebrities, pop idols and an online pitchfork mob versus scientific caution. A popular movement known as Blue Flag sprang up. Its adherents dyed their hair bright blue and wore blue clothing. Some painted their faces and even bodies blue, not unlike the ancient warriors of Britain. The Blue Flag swelled and swept the Earth, banners aloft. Its adherents, who became increasingly zealous, said it was the sacred duty of humanity to welcome this lifeform to Earth. As for any risks scientists might say it posed, they retorted that other scientists – admittedly far fewer in number – were certain that with thorough measures taken it could never pose a risk to humanity. There were demonstrations for and against. Some turned into riots. Politicians and political parties got involved. It swung elections, governments rose and fell. And in the end, the Blue Flag prevailed, celebrating with global concerts, street festivals and revelry.

The most secure facility ever constructed was built in the deepest, still frozen reaches of Antarctica, and the most bio-secure spacecraft dispatched to collect it. On board was a lab with so many layers of security it was exhausting for scientists to get inside it and work. And so it came to pass that the slime was loaded on Mars, blasted off and reached Earth safely. Its arrival was greeted by the joyous millions, and billions more online around the world. Everyone went mad for blue: blue models, blue celebrities, blue parties, blue mass orgies and blue rock bands that played stadium anthems, novelty and kiddie pop, in fact everything but the blues.

Once it was installed in the facility, the scientists went to work. One thing they quickly discovered was that the most minute of signals – chemical-electric impulses undetectable to all but the most finely tuned of instruments – were buzzing constantly within it. At first these were surmised to be cellular signals, although it had still not been established that it even had cells, but as testing proceeded and became ever more finely calibrated and the level of sophistication of internal signalling became apparent, a staggering conclusion was announced to the world. Far from being a mere cowpat-shaped blob of slime, the electric blue organism appeared most closely to resemble a large, highly sophisticated brain. It was a brain without a body, a brain whose "thoughts" no-one could read, but the inescapable conclusion had to be that it was indeed "thinking". All of Earth and the colony on Mars went into a kind of collective shock. This thing was *intelligent??* What was going on, humanity wondered? What was it doing and what did it want? And all the while the Brain, as it was immediately dubbed, sat there in its glass case, feeding on its diet of CO_2, filtered artificial sunlight and trace water vapour. It did nothing, it seemed, but "think", if indeed that human concept accurately described what it was doing. Papers were published positing various theories. One was the Brain had its own conception of time and perhaps this was but a moment for it in which it was doing nothing. Another argued it was waiting, possibly for an opportunity. Yet another said it was asleep, and all the brain activity was "dreaming".

The longer this went on, the more fascinated yet bewildered the scientists became, and with them all humanity. Meanwhile the online world embraced it to a whole new level. Netizens enjoyed virtual realities in which they got to "say hello" to the Brain. They could chat to it, confess to it if they were so inclined, virtual-touch it, even "have sex" with it. Soon the Brain was everywhere, projected onto the sides of buildings, of mountains, across the wide night sky. People flocked for robo-cosmetic surgery to have their eyeballs turned electric blue. Some had their bodies tattooed face to toe with it and became known as Blue People. Just when it seemed no fad could top the last, it did. Corporations grew ever richer on ideas to "blue" your lifestyle: blue genitals, blue tongues, blue homes, whole blue cities. Blue, blue, blue was all, on the Blue Planet as well as the Red. And all along the Brain sat unmoving, immutable, inscrutable, and blue.

The morning came when the world awoke to the shock news that a terrorist cell had attempted a break-in to steal the Brain in a plot to ransom it for a chunk of the wealth of the Earth. They were only repelled at the last line of defence by guards. Fragments from one blast even penetrated to the very last layer of glass. Despite their relief at the theft being foiled, scientists worried the Brain might have been disturbed and physically or "psychologically" harmed.

Nothing happened. The Brain sat in its glass case unchanged, buzzing away with its opaque, tiny impulses. After the plotters were all caught and jailed, it was decided that the remote location was a risk as the terrorists had outnumbered the defenders and it took too long for reinforcements to arrive. The Brain had almost been stolen. Worse, it could have died. It had to be moved to a more central secure location.

The United States argued the Brain rightly belonged to it, as it had been an American who first colonised Mars. Britain said Dee Jones, who found it, was a British citizen and it rightly belonged there. Other countries clamoured with their own reasons. Eventually it became a decision of the United Nations, and after raucous, even rancorous debate, it voted. The Brain would go to the Smithsonian Institution in Washington.

A new ultra-secure wing was constructed. As well as labs and security, it included a massive Viewing Room, as American politicians argued it was every US citizen's God-given right to see the Brain. That instantly became another thorny international dispute and it was promptly extended to "every person's God-given right". The Viewing Room could handle ten thousand people in a four-hour Viewing Session each day, and there was more global celebration when the Brain, in its specially engineered bullet- and blast-proof glass sarcophagus, had its first public display and the influx of "Brain Tourists" began, eager for their very own 1.5 second walk by at 20 metres' distance from the sarcophagus which was protected behind a floor-to-ceiling blast-proof glass wall.

The global online community was momentarily mollified. Everyone could have the chance to see the Brain, they appeared to reason, until someone did the maths on how long it would take for the billions on Earth to view it and realised that even with science extending lifespans, the vast majority of people would never see it, because if you were at the back of the queue it could take you 2700 years to reach the Viewing Room. This sparked yet another furore over equality of viewing opportunity, or EVO as it became called. It was just more of the hegemony of the tech oligarchs and rich countries, the poorer countries argued. Everyone on Earth, no matter who or where they lived, clime or class, must have the right to a viewing. The Brain had to be on display for a longer time each day, people argued. But the scientists ruled that was too big a risk. They did not know if it would "tire", but it could well do. And even with longer hours it could still take hundreds, even a thousand years to see it anyway.

Lotteries were proposed for viewings. Inevitably there was widespread corruption and equally inevitably the celebrity elite got private VIP viewings, even if these generated red-carpet pix more than resentment. So there were two paths: win or rig a lottery, or become a celebrity in a world already awash with them.

A further complication came with a flowering of cults centred on the Brain. A plethora of online myths sprang up, propagated by conspiracies, memes, rumours, chat. Some claimed that merely glimpsing the Brain could impart greater intelligence, even "cosmic consciousness" (although what that was remained moot). Others argued a viewing could make the viewer superhuman, even a demigod, adding to popular pressure for more hours. Despite scientists pleading for common sense, pointing out that those who had been longest and closest with it remained mere fallible mortals, in the fevered online realm, where the mass of humanity dwelled, the cults spread like a blue rash across the world.

One of these was headed by a charismatic young man with dark flowing locks and whole-body blue tattooing known as Finnegan. The central dogma of Finneganism was simple: the Brain was God. In this case it was the God that humans had yearned for throughout history, an eternal, immutable, all-knowing, wise and benign deity in which to invest all the trust of our lost selves. Finneganism almost instantly gained an evangelical fervour. First it had millions of faithful, then hundreds of millions, soon billions. The entire Earth was gripped by a new, ever wilder mania for the Brain. Crowds as far as the eye could see thronged Washington. Troubles inevitably broke out and spread. Hundreds were crushed daily as they clamoured, pushed and shoved to get near the Smithsonian, many falling beneath the heels of the seething mob, never to be seen again as ever more surged on to try to reach the holy place.

Finnegan did his best to hold them back, until even he was killed in one particularly mad and brutal crush. The authorities did what they could. Mostly troops fired tear gas and water cannon, but increasingly they resorted to live ammunition. Occasionally some in the crowds fired back. Often in the heat and confusion and choking chaos of so much human flesh jammed into limited urban space, it felt as if the world would explode and descend into anarchy and civil war. Each time the authorities managed to regain order, but only just.

Then came the Great Schism, when a dissenting faction of Finneganism under a Tongan oracle named Liliko sprang up. The difference in dogma was definitive. Lilikism also posited that the Brain was God, but held that the divine Brain could see into the soul of every person, and required genuine repentance for sin, as well as a divesting of all corrupting material wealth, in return for the revelation of the meaning of one's life. A global bonfire of the vanities ensued in which vast mobs torched all their possessions in immense "Holy Blazes" in the streets and then subsisted in the empty shells of their homes to try to make themselves worthy of the revelation to come from the Brain.

To complicate things even further, a counter-movement emerged: the Red People. The Reds sprang up when the United States elected a buffoon to end all buffoons as its leader, a village idiot who could barely think, much less reason. But President Thelma Cubit had enormous sway among the poorer and less educated, and she seized the opportunity to champion the Red cause and became a global celebrity. The Reds saw the Brain as a dangerous, even satanic entity and wanted it returned to Mars. The extreme Red faction even wanted it destroyed. This movement spread quickly too. It swept up those who felt resentful and threatened by a Brain they could never see in their lifetimes anyway, and that just sat there and did nothing but "think" about things no-one could understand. Who knew what it might be cooking up? Control of the world? The end of humanity?

Incited by the ranting speeches of President Cubit, tensions escalated. The day came when millions of followers of all three groups converged on Washington. The Finneganist and Lilikist factions decided they needed to put aside their dogmatic differences for the greater struggle of the Blues against the lunatic Reds. Despite a nationwide call-up, the security forces were hopelessly outnumbered and soon all they could do was watch as the largest hand-to-hand battle in human history was fought out on the streets of Washington.

It began with banter, name calling, shouting on the front lines. A few skirmishes broke out, fist fights turned into melees. Knuckles and sticks escalated to clubs, knives, axes and then guns. Immense running battles raged throughout the city. Buildings burned. Tens of thousands fell to the bullet, the blade, or were trampled to death in front of the White House, on the steps of the Capitol or in a massive clash of lines of tens of thousands charging up and down the National Mall. The battles raged for days with passions unabated.

Just when it seemed as if it might die down and the police and troops get the upper hand, a thrust of a few hundred diehard Reds unexpectedly breached safety lines, then the final layers of security, and swarmed upon the sarcophagus holding the Brain, intent on its destruction. Before they could be stopped they took axes and clubs to it, and by the time they were beaten back the supposedly blast-proof glass case had been smashed open and fragments of glass had fallen onto the Brain inside. There was even a blow delivered to the Brain itself by a large trident, by a man daubed in Red wearing devil horns. As police rounded up the Reds, Liliko herself crept in unseen, reached out and touched the wounded Brain, stroking it with her bare, healing fingers before being pulled away by horrified scientists.

Word spread through the immense crowd about what had happened and millions were stilled and silenced. In that terrible moment the people of the Earth feared they had committed the most abominable of crimes. They had murdered God.

The Earth fell silent. Recovery teams collected the bodies and the streets were cleansed. The crowds returned to their homes. A profound sense of remorse and ever deeper guilt set in. Liliko solemnly pronounced it the Second Original Sin. Only it was far, far worse. The First Original Sin was from a legend recorded in antiquity but this had occurred in their own lives, recorded before the naked eye of all the world's media, indisputable, an appalling felony, and so many of them had taken part in it. The man who had swung the trident was sentenced to the term of his natural life working down the toughest mine on Mars. President Cubit, who had incited him and the rest of the Reds, was acquitted at her fourth impeachment, on party lines.

Meanwhile the scientists rehoused the Brain and security was reinforced yet again. They observed. They scanned. They considered. There was a clear gap in the creature left by the blow of the trident. Yet like human skin after a wound, by the millimetre the sides began to creep together, and it appeared to "heal". Even more remarkably, it seemed to have survived full exposure to the alien atmosphere of Earth. There was no discernible difference in the Brain at all. Its colour and vividness were unchanged despite the fears of the scientists that any diminution or fading would be a sign of "infection", even of impending death. Instead, by degree the Brain reconstituted and within a few weeks was fully itself again, buzzing with its micro-signals. The scientists, the politicians, the people of two planets breathed a collective sigh of relief. God was not dead after all! "God lives!!" they cried on the streets.

There were jubilant celebrations for weeks and for the mass of humanity the divinity of the Brain was confirmed: that it could survive a trident blow while exposed to an alien atmosphere proved it beyond doubt. Delivered from the mortal sin of murder, they were delighted to see the Brain seemingly well, and gave thanks in prayer sessions attended by millions and screened across the globe. These were led by Liliko who, being the only human ever to have touched the Brain with her own body, was now known as "the Vestal".

There were no more floods of people into Washington. Now only the lottery winners came and waited in an orderly, respectful line. An international commission cleaned up the lottery system and laid the blame for their former corruption on President Cubit and her shady associates, and she was impeached yet again. As the world looked on, it felt as if things at last were getting better.

But then something else unusual happened.

After research resumed, the scientists were able to confirm that despite being exposed to the atmosphere of Earth, with its preponderance of nitrogen and richness in oxygen, the Brain appeared not only to be unharmed but unaffected in any way. Astoundingly, it seemed to have fully recovered from its wound and to have coped perfectly well with at least half an hour of full exposure to the atmosphere of a different planet.

What was going on?

Science didn't know.

Conspiracy theories threatened to run riot again but the once-bitten

Earth was twice shy. This time the mass of people waited for the scientists to speak. And when they did, the world was astonished by what they said.

The Brain seemed to be growing.

Was it possible, some speculated, that it had been stimulated by its exposure to the atmosphere of Earth? The scientists had of course returned it immediately to its Mars-replicant atmosphere, but had its exposure tripped some "switch" in it? Others theorised it was swollen by the wound, and now that it had recovered, over time it would revert to its original size.

But it didn't. It kept growing.

Scientists were ever more deeply puzzled. What was going on? Then one wrote a paper positing what was seen by many colleagues as a dangerously far-fetched theory: the Brain had tasted the atmosphere of Earth, liked it, and was "hungry" for more.

Few took it seriously. Even if the Brain grew a little more, it could be readily contained. A month passed. During that time it kept growing, just a little. Publicly, there was reassurance the growth was of little consequence, but behind the scenes, top secret plans were drawn up. If it did keep growing and presented any kind of threat, it would be deprived of its life sources… CO_2, water vapour, sunlight… and killed. One did not gamble with the fate of the Earth.

But it did keep growing. The population of Earth saw it live 24/7 on their screens. Public opinion on how to respond was divided. Some ranted it should be killed, now, by deprivation, blast or flame. Others pleaded for its life, including Liliko and her followers. As with nearly every issue to do with the Brain, scientists were divided. They knew prudence dictated its life support should be switched off. Yet the spirit of scientific enquiry said it must be allowed to survive if at all possible, as the unique creature it was. One faction strongly argued it should be returned to Mars, to the exact crevice where it was found. After all, what right did humanity have to take it from Mars to Earth, and then kill it? Again, it would be murder, not of God of course, as the netizen nuts still thought it was, but of an entity that had every right to its existence in nature, on its home world.

A scientific compromise was proposed. Life support would be turned off, but only for a few seconds, to see if that could stop the growth. Instruments would measure electrical pulses while the Brain was plunged into darkness and denied CO2 and water vapour. Despite the deepest of misgivings, the greatest minds in science agreed, ignoring the pleas of the Vestal. Most of the world's leaders concurred, ignoring the demands of President Cubit for instant incineration.

The day came, then the moment. A hooded scientist dubbed "the Executioner" by the Vestal and much of the online realm, touched a button that switched off the Brain's life support. Ten seconds later, they switched it back on. Scientists frantically scanned the results as they flashed up on the screen. Astonishingly, astoundingly, nothing had happened. Growth had gone on unimpeded despite being deprived of sunlight. Over the days and weeks that followed, the scientists searched for an explanation and came to something of a consensus, however bizarre it might seem. The theory was that the Brain was able to "flip" from photosynthesis to other life processes. The shocking corollary was that rather than being what humans understood as from the plant domain, it was also from the animal. The Brain was both.

Scientists were yet again stunned. For the followers of the Vestal and the netizen nuts, it was the final, undeniable confirmation that the Brain was God.

Then one scientist spoke up and fought to be heard. 'If being deprived of what it needs for survival has no discernible effect on it, then what would it take to kill it?'

'Exactly!' the Vestal cried out to the watching global masses. 'The Brain is immortal, eternal God!!'

Within weeks, the Brain outgrew its glass sarcophagus. Scientists were still debating whether to transfer it to a larger containment when, with a sudden, unexpected growth spurt, the sarcophagus shattered and the Brain oozed out into the laboratory. Scientists fell back in terror as it spread across the floor forming a blue carpet, with little clumps throughout, which they later thought must be crucial interchanges, brain centres. The scientists secured the facility, at the rear of the Smithsonian, but now with access to air, the Brain seemed to grow much more quickly and soon burst out of the facility in a throbbing blue tide.

Scientists pleaded for time to get it under control. The Blues rushed to worship it, the Reds to kill it. Police again struggled to keep the warring factions apart. President Cubit ordered an immediate nuclear strike on it, until the Pentagon pointed out that would vaporise Washington, including the White House where she sat behind the Resolute Desk.

Now it spread with terrifying speed. Within days, it had covered all of Washington, with just the Monument poking up through the tide of blue slime. As it went on, scientists concluded the wave did not actively seek to kill or hurt, it merely spread. Yet below its tide, vegetation and creatures, including people who failed to leave in time, were inevitably asphyxiated.

The military took over the response. Tanks and artillery fired shells. Aircraft flew precision bombing missions. The munitions left a gap in the blue tide, which promptly mended itself as it flowed on into West Virginia. Just as panic was taking root across the Earth, scientists observed another twist: the rate of spread appeared to be slowing. Had it been hurt after all by the attacks? That was one view, but the Vestal intoned what many others suspected. 'The Brain is giving us time to leave,' she sang, declaring it had now permitted her to join in a "holy communion" with its thoughts.

With the lull, the generals argued now was the time to strike and kill it once and for all. The military pulled out all the tricks in its box. Chemical weapons. Biological. Cyber. Massive lasers. All to no avail. Finally, against the pleadings of the scientists, the generals launched an immense co-ordinated attack of nuclear warheads with enough combined destructive force to blow it off the face of the Earth. And it did. The problem was that everywhere that fragments, even particles of it came down in the fallout, they gathered into vivid blue radioactive puddles that pooled into lakes, and the Brain reconstituted itself – but spreading much, much more quickly now – and emitting lethal radiation. The message the Vestal translated from the Brain was "if you continue doing this, it will only speed my spread, and make me even more deadly to yourselves". She pleaded for reason to prevail.

Scientific observations continued. It was confirmed that it did not cover seas: it stopped at the shores, which meant the oceans and their creatures might survive, especially if there was no further increase in radiation. It was not known how it would cross oceans, but it was feared nonetheless that somehow every inch of the land mass of Earth would in time be covered.

Meanwhile, President Cubit raved that she had a 'secret ultimate weapon' that she promised would 'take the fucker out'. But most world leaders ignored her ever more deranged rants and began planning a human escape to Mars. So much depended on the rate of the spread. If it slowed enough, there might just be time to get a small but potentially viable population to Mars.

Cubit was overthrown and jailed in a federal prison that was covered in a sudden and unexpected surge of slime a month later. The new US administration joined the world in planning a mass migration as quickly as possible. Attempts to destroy the Brain ended. And when they did, its spread slowed again. It grew by feet per day, not miles. 'The Brain has given humanity ten years to leave,' the Vestal sang. By now the world, even its leaders, accepted her word, especially as the slime spared the space launch facilities.

A decade may seem a long time, but everyone knew now it was less than a moment. At the same time, the billions on Earth were squeezed ever more closely together, after the Brain crossed the Panama Canal and then the Bering Strait. Scientists theorised it used something equivalent to spores to accomplish water crossings, and when local communities tried to stamp out new colonies with fire and explosives, again they only spread it more quickly. In time, it was on all continents.

Lotteries were held for the desperately rare seats to leave as workers laboured around the clock to rush the production of the huge fleet of spacecraft to ferry them and the building materials for the settlements in which they would live. Other human communities were trialled in the Earth's oceans. Some of these seemed viable, others fell quickly to violent radioactive storms, as well as to social discord and mental illness among people unable to adapt to living so far from land.

Over the decade, spacecraft ferried as many people as possible – inevitably the political leadership, trillionaires and then billionaires had priority – to Mars. Settlements were built at a frantic pace. Many were defective, and the new occupants perished as walls were punctured or collapsed, or equipment broke down or exploded. There were concerns, then alarm, as corners were cut too with insulation against radiation, and some of the lava tubes being used for exclusive underground havens for the wealthiest collapsed, burying everyone inside alive. There were other worries, that people in the long run would not survive, physically but also mentally, in such a harsh, barren, unforgiving world. Nonetheless the frantic migration and construction work went on unabated. About half a billion people were also now in settlements out in the Earth's oceans, but their survival was proving almost as precarious as for those on Mars.

On the day the ten years expired, the Brain began to grow more rapidly and in the space of a few years – during which tens of thousands more managed the scramble off the planet to Mars – it covered the entire land-mass of the Earth. The only humans to remain living on it then were the surviving ocean colonists and those hardy enough to dwell in the thin air and cold of the tall peaks, the mountain people of places like Tibet, Nepal, the European Alps, the Rockies, the Andes, and Kilimanjaro.

The Vestal was among the last to leave. She took a parting message from the Brain but said now was not the time to reveal it.

Ten Earth years later, Dee Jones and Tora Lindvig joined the Vestal in a live transmission to all the communities of Mars. They looked back at the Earth up in the night sky, a glittering blue gem on the black velvet of space. It was left to Dee to pose the question all of surviving humanity wished to ask, as they huddled cold and hungry in their half-insulated shelters, contemplating a life of endless struggle to survive on Mars and lament their paradise lost.

'What was the Brain's message to parting humanity? Dee asked the Vestal.

The Vestal sang: 'It said thank you for your beautiful planet.'

So ends my account of this tragic episode in the history of our species. Other than the few who persist on the peaks and high seas of Earth, we are now an expatriate race, in exile. Mars is our home, for good or ill, mostly ill. Every night we humans look up at the sky and see the glimmer of our glorious blue Earth and weep at our folly of losing it.

As the Vestal intoned to humanity as the transmission ended: 'Look into the mirror, and do more than reflect.'

Sonya Nyerere
History House, ElonGate.

The Society

She woke early on her birthday. The birds were calling in the garden as dawn crept around the blinds. He snored on beside her, his soft, whinnying snore. As she lay in bed, in the warmth of nothing to do, she was thinking of mortality. Not so surprising on a birthday: another year on the clock. Mortality, eternity, infinity have ever voided the mind, she reflected. Time and space without end challenge logic and reason, just as humanity knew it faced the obverse: a finite span punctuated by death, non-existence. People had tried to make sense of it as best they could of course, she knew, creating religions and philosophies and formulating scientific theories of time and space, even of parallel universes and realities, although somehow these didn't help much when you were stuck in the one you were in. And yet, she considered as she lay there, had not mortality marked humanity as different from its gods, even superior in a way, as human follies passed into time while those of the fickle, irascible gods were eternal.

She slipped on her robe and went barefoot from the room. There was an early stillness through the house that she loved, in the muted fall of foot as if on trimmed turf. The glass wall of the living room gave its green and pleasant vista of the woods behind. She picked out her favourite tree, the Japanese maple, in full leaf, perfection of form and balance. She tucked her feet up under her on the sofa and gazed out, and wondered if the purpose of her existence was to admire this tree: in which case, what did it mean if she outlived it?

She put the kettle on for tea. There was a congenial ritual to its preparation that was considered beneficial. It framed the day, as did meals and drinks. The kettle was a vintage whistler she liked. She warmed the pot and put in two teaspoons in case he woke and wanted a cup. She poured in the boiling water, the vapour twitching her nose, found the tea cosy she had knitted with the big ruby strawberries on top, cloaked the pot and waited for the tea to draw. She took her time: it was her birthday after all, and there was no need to hurry, not that there ever really was anyway. She poured the tea into her favourite cup, the cornflower blue one, delicate as a nautilus shell, with the white seaside daisy pattern on it, added a dash of milk and went outside.

It was a wonderfully cool morning in the hills. Rags of mist lay forgotten in the crooks of valleys. The treetops were stilled, and above them in the hazy early light the clouds curled in dreaming pillows. Gems of dew adorned pine needles. The steam from her cup rose and drifted off like half a question. There was so much time, for everything, for the steam to dissipate before her eyes, and to watch each tendril fade. She sipped, the cup warming her hand. When finished she set it down on the garden table where they had their wine at dusk, and walked down the garden.

She reached out to the maple and touched its trunk as one might the cheek of a lover. How could something so old still be so sapling smooth, as if it could be young forever? Her trailing fingers left it and she meandered on, along the narrow path with the forest thick and lush by either shoulder. She felt the humus and soft shreds of bark beneath her toes and thought that was how it was to love.

As she strolled, she wondered again how they filled up all the hours. There was an endless horizon of them: days, years, decades. What did they do with all that? They ate, read, walked in the woods, watched films: she wrote poems and he took photographs. They devoted a lot of time to selecting wines and pored over vintage recipes. They read, they played squash and swam in the pool. They worked in the garden and watched the roses bud, bloom and shrivel to hips. They mulched, composted, grafted and pruned. They enjoyed their own potatoes, tomatoes and plums. Sometimes they made love, other times they went on picnics. They travelled all over the planet, even ascended Olympus Mons. They visited friends across the valley or in town, and sometimes friends came to dinner and they would talk into the small hours of politics and authors, and joke about some silly new fad in art. Later, the two of them would sit and pick back over it all. It was engaging, nice and passed the time. There was time for it all, and all in time. Nothing was ever early or late: things happened, and the time passed. But there was so much of it, with unimaginably more to come.

She followed the pathway down through the woods. Animals including leopards, dingoes, bears and wolves were increasing in numbers and could well be about, not that that was any real concern. They delighted in their presence and duly reported their sightings. She threw back her head and looked up. If you peered very closely you could see the ultrafine membrane of their region's biodome. Beyond it, two tiny moons whirled around their planet. Winding to the bottom of the valley, the path led to their little stream, and she lingered by it. She touched the moss on a log. It was so soft it tingled her fingertips. She dangled her toes in the stream and giggled at how icy it was. As she did, the encrypted message she had been expecting came in from the Society. Her gift was on its way. 'Happy Birthday', the Chair said.

She crossed the stream at the stepping stones and went on, climbing the far bank. There was another stand of trees there, these ones huge-trunked, towering, with a dense canopy. They called it their own Wild Wood, from *The Wind in the Willows*. She had loved reading the book to the children, so long ago. "'Beyond the Wild Wood Comes the Wide World,' said the Rat."

She padded along the path, through the dark, dank, wonderfully musty-sour smelling heart of the wood until she saw what they called "the hatch" up ahead, the rectangle of light at the far end, and stepped out through it into the sun on the lofty rock ledge beyond it, just three or four paces short of the edge. The view was wondrous here, a joy, across the valley to the grand stone bluffs on the far side, brushed soft peach and rose by the early light. The drop-off was spectacular in itself, sheer and straight down to the rocks far below. It was always a bit dizzying to stand by that edge, even if in reality there was nothing to fear.

She felt powerful arms encircle her from behind.

'Early,' he said, nuzzling into her neck.

She kept looking across to the bluffs. 'I'm so very happy darling.'

'Good. And just for the record, you are also so very beautiful.'

She turned around to him. 'Are you sure?' she teased.

'Your body might be a twenty-year-old, but you still look wonderful as ever.'

'I thought you might think it's time for a new body. For us both perhaps now.'

'Not yet,' he said. 'We've barely run these in. And haven't you seen the latest models? No? The new skin is amazingly soft and supple, true... but the Cheat-Up features, the plumped lips and bulbous breasts... the bulging pecs... I thought we were past all that.'

'Some things we're never past.'

He kissed her. They had been together back to when they both had hearts and bones, for so long now that friends good-naturedly gossiped. They didn't care.

'Happy birthday darling.'

'Thank you,' she said.

'And the big 200 coming next year, eh.'

She nodded and smiled. She knew that in that moment the last of her memory banks and all their backups were being secretly hacked and deleted from every single secure official data storage simultaneously, by her friends in the Society. Soon all that remained of "her" would comprise the tiny mineral webwork inside her carbon-fibre cranium. And that cranium was strong, it was true, but no match for rock.

'I'm making you a special birthday breakfast,' he said. 'Come on.'

'You go on ahead, darling.'

He paused, shrugged, gave her his smile and started walking back. He knew her.

'I just want to admire the view one moment more,' she said, as he went back through the hatch.

Afterword

There is an array of responses to the notion of the human colonisation of Mars. One of the most common views is that it is preposterous even to try to get there, much less settle it. The argument goes that there are so many other things that need to be fixed on Earth first. While this may seep with common sense, there will always be things that need to be fixed on Earth, and fixing them first is not historically how we as a species have operated. We've always left our mess behind us for some daydream El Dorado just over the horizon. Other people see a Mars shift as inevitable, especially given the climate crisis, the wrath of which we have only just begun to feel, with at least some of our planet probably becoming uninhabitable over coming decades. Others again see it almost as a necessity, a kind of species outreach, a "human pioneering spirit" which must continue if we truly are to evolve.

What will happen remains unclear. But given our history, it seems likely there will at least be an attempt to get humans to Mars, and possibly establish some kind of permanent presence there. Finding water is a key to any settlement plan, and indications of underground ice mean that fundamental problem may be resolved. Radiation too – barely a problem on Earth – could be a major concern for settlers, and demand endless precautions and countermeasures. Then there is the simply immense distance involved, and the time and effort involved in Martian travel. So what could take us to Mars, beyond "Because it's there"?

Finding rare minerals could be a strong incentive, although these would need to be extremely valuable to be worth the cost of the fuel to fly them back in the ships delivering settlers and supplies from Earth. The search for life on Mars in some form or other will go on too, and any results could well challenge our notions of what "life" is. With its gargantuan peaks and bleak, austere vistas, and with the Earth backpacked, packaged-toured and cruised to death, Martian tourism could become an industry of its own.

Obviously so much about any human future on Mars remains speculation, in the vein of last century's Golden Age of Science Fiction. After all, we are still trying to put together the first human expedition there. But if we do go and decide to set up a permanent human presence, the effects on those who depart and those who remain will be profound. Humanity has experienced the "tyranny of distance" before; but this tyranny will be total, the isolation near-complete. Some will find it impossible, while a few may find the freedom exhilarating. For most it could be drudgery, a sentence to be endured. But the effects on the consciousness and psyche of all who go, and those they leave behind, will be deep and lasting.

For all intents and purposes, Mars is the only other planet in our solar system we could conceivably inhabit. Although a rocky planet, Venus has a surface temperature and an atmosphere too inhospitable to contemplate human presence. Half of Mercury is fried by the Sun and the other half frozen, and Jupiter and Saturn are gas giants. Some hope is held out for their moons, but these are almost impossibly distant from Earth with our current technology. So practically, Mars is it for us – our first and last planetary outpost, beyond our Moon.

It might seem an ultimate folly even to contemplate colonising Mars, but with our track record as a species, it seems if we can do it, we will. And while space tycoon Elon Musk continues to be a controversial figure, a crank to some, and to others a visionary, and perhaps both to others still, we must remember that those who take our species to new places and times are often seen as that. Whatever the case, it must be said he has put reaching and future colonisation of Mars well and truly on our human agenda, and so would deserve any first settlement there to bear his name.

Larry Buttrose

Leura, New South Wales, 2024.